D1328217

ANNIE'S ATTIC MYSTERIES®

The
Wedding
Dress

Mary O'Donnell

AnniesMysteries.com

Library of Congress-in-Publication Data
The Wedding Dress / by Mary O'Donnell
p. cm.
I. Title
                              2011909878

AnniesMysteries.com
800-282-6643
Annie's Attic Mysteries®
Series Creator: Stenhouse & Associates, Ridgefield, Connecticut
Series Editors: Ken and Janice Tate

10 11 12 13 14 | Printed in China | 10 9 8 7 6 5 4 3 2 1

— *Dedication* —

To the women in my life who have taught me so much: my grandmothers, Ida and Myrtle; my mother, Pat; my sisters, Doris and Becky; and my daughter, Julie.

"The web of our life is of a mingled yarn, good and ill together." —William Shakespeare

— Prologue —

On a bright spring day in 1895, Captain Zacharias Grey stood atop a high hill overlooking the rocky coast of Maine. Behind him, the remains of the previous year's tall grass, brown and flattened by the wind and by layer upon layer of winter snow, were being pushed aside as new sprouts of green plants took over. The deciduous trees were budding, the leaves nearly ready to burst forth after a long, cold and dark winter, and the branches of the pines were tipped in the light green of new growth. Soon wildflowers would open their petals and dot the landscape with color— yellow marsh marigold and golden Alexanders, purple spiderwort, red columbine, deep blue lupine and light blue Jacob's ladder.

Before the captain lay the ocean; that day it was a deep blue color, reflecting the clear blue sky above. In his many years at sea, he had seen the ocean in a range of colors and moods from black as night, to iron gray, to the sparkling blue he saw before him. The wind was blowing briskly inland at about 10 to 12 knots, he had calculated, both by the feel of it on his hands and face, and by the appearance of white caps on the waves. The air was cold and full of the smell of the sea.

He loved the sea. It had been his life since he had left home as a young man—a boy really, only 17 years old—to work as a seaman on his first voyage aboard a merchant vessel. By the age of 22, he had worked his way up to second mate, and from there he proceeded to higher ranks. With each advancement in experience and responsibility he garnered a larger share of the profit. Fifteen years after he stepped foot on that first ship as a simple seaman, he was a captain, and soon he hoped to be co-owner of his own ship.

It was not a foregone conclusion that he would achieve his goals. There were many men, older than he, who remained seaman, or rose to second or first mate, but no further. He had the good fortune to be born with a mind adept at learning, and he had had mentors along the way who taught him not only the craft of seafaring, but lent him books to further the education that had been cut short when he took to the sea.

The sea captains of that age were learned men. They did not normally socialize with the crew and spent long hours alone in the evenings and on days when there was a lull of activity. Reading was a way to pass the time and expand their knowledge. Under the tutelage of a few of these men, young Zacharias Grey studied the fundamentals of learning—grammar, logic, arithmetic, geometry— so that he might advance to study higher things. He read with relish stories like Homer's *Odyssey* and Shakespeare's *Tempest*. The understanding of astronomy that was fundamental to sailing was expanded to a greater understanding of the earth's place in the sea of the universe. His goal was to be able to hold his own in conversation with those with whom he hoped to become a peer, but he was enriched beyond his expectation.

Now in his mid-30s, Captain Grey envisioned his plans for the future as he watched the gulls sail high into the air off the shore of the small town of Stony Point. He had purchased the outcrop of land where he was standing, where there would soon be built a fine home for himself and his young bride-to-be, who was herself from a Boston family of long-standing. In their new home, they would raise the large family they wanted to have. It would be the first house built along what had formerly been an earthen track, only recently having been paved with brick and christened "Ocean Drive."

An architect from Boston had been engaged to draw up plans for a large, many-gabled house featuring a wraparound porch, with a carriage house situated nearby. The carriage house had already been started, and soon the builders would break ground to begin the main house. Captain Grey estimated that by the time he returned from his next commercial voyage, the house would be complete. After a honeymoon in Europe, he would bring his bride to live in Stony Point. She might accompany him on some of his voyages, if she liked, before the children were born. He could see the future laid out before him in his mind's eye.

He had decided he would give the house a name, like some of the grand places he had seen in his travels to England—with names like Holkham Hall, Sandringham House and Mentmore Towers. He knew that his house would not be palatial like those magnificent buildings, but nevertheless his home would be one of the finest houses in Stony Point. The name he had chosen was Grey Gables.

$$- \mathcal{1} -$$

$\mathcal{A}$nnie Dawson awoke early in the morning with a sense of resolve that she was really going to make some progress in the attic that day. She had been in Stony Point, Maine, for quite a while, living in the house that her grandmother, Elizabeth "Betsy" Holden, had bequeathed to her. Annie had made the long drive up from her home in Brookfield, Texas, with a mission: to put things in order, and then return as soon as possible. Her beloved husband Wayne had passed away, but her daughter, LeeAnn, still lived in Texas with her husband, Herb, and their twin children, Joanna and John. Annie also had many wonderful friends she had come to know and love over the years. But when she arrived at her grandmother's home, Grey Gables, she found that there was so much more to do than she had expected.

The house had fallen into a certain amount of disrepair, as her grandmother, in her later years, was unable to keep up with all that goes with maintaining a large house. The old Victorian-period house had been her grandparents' home since the 1940s. When Annie's grandfather had died, her grandmother couldn't bear to "downsize" like other widows often do out of necessity. She stayed at Grey Gables, the home where she had lived since she was a young wife and mother, living daily with memories of the people she had loved and cared for, and continuing to reach out to her friends and neighbors. Annie loved the house too. She had spent her summers with Gram, as she liked to call her grandmother, from the time when she was a child until she went away to college.

But time had passed so quickly. After college, Annie had married, and she and Wayne worked long hours to establish their business, a car dealership, in Texas. And then LeeAnn was born. ... Annie just never seemed to find the time to go to Maine. The last time she was there was to attend her grandfather's funeral. After that, it was easier to arrange to fly Gram down to Texas for holidays or special occasions. Being so far away, Annie hadn't realized that Grey Gables had become too much for her grandmother to handle.

When Annie arrived in Stony Point, she quickly saw that she had her work cut out for her. She was not a do-it-yourself kind of girl when it came to home repairs, but fortunately, she found a great handyman in Wally Carson, who was helping her get things in shape. She and Wally had made progress in nearly every part of the house. Slowly, Annie was working her way through each of the rooms, keeping the feel of the home she remembered as a child, but applying her own sense of style as an organizing principle. She thought that Gram would approve.

And then there was the attic. Annie sighed deeply just thinking about it. As she lay in bed, watching the first sunbeams of another summer day stream through lacy crocheted curtains, she knew that today was the day when she was really going to see a significant change in the attic. It was the one part of the house where she just hadn't seemed to be able to make any headway. But today would be different.

She had asked Wally to come by to do some electrical work in the attic. He would remove the old ceiling fixture, with its bare lightbulb and dangling pull string, and install new lighting fixtures and outlets that Annie had picked out the previous week at Malone's Hardware Store. She hoped that the new lighting would give her a needed boost, as she sorted through all of the miscellanea in the attic.

Her immediate impression, after she arrived from Texas and wandered up into the attic for the first time in nearly 30 years, was "clutter and dust." After that, she always went up the narrow stairs into the attic with the intention of getting everything cleaned and organized. The dust she could deal with, but the clutter was complicated. Without fail she found that she was distracted from her organizational goal by some unexpected treasure. No, it wasn't always something that belonged on *Antiques Roadshow*—though some of the things she had found certainly did. Other items, while not antiques, were valuable nonetheless, and not just monetarily. She thought of the first "treasure" she discovered—her grandmother's "Betsy Original," an embroidered portrait of a mysterious lady. Even mundane articles that seemed at first to be the antithesis of "mysterious," often turned out to be clues that led to all different sorts of long-buried secrets that Annie had helped to see the light of day, and in the process she had ultimately helped those who were connected.

Each "treasure" that she came across had a unique aura. As she held the object in her hands, it seemed to "tell" her that it had an interesting and important history of its own, and that it was her duty to uncover it. She just couldn't pack everything in boxes and take them down to the secondhand shopz or to the church rummage sale to get rid of them. She felt she owed an obligation to her grandmother who had saved these precious things, and to the people who had been associated with them, to discover that special history. Somehow she would make sure each item was where it should be, and that any loose ends associated with it were resolved. Her grandparents and her parents had engrained into her the idea that she should care for others, even strangers, and she took that idea seriously.

Her friends at the Hook and Needle Club liked to call her attempts to discover the stories behind her attic treasures her "mysteries," and were almost always eager to lend a hand to solve the mystery at hand. Annie smiled as she thought of the ladies, who got together as a group every Tuesday morning at the local needlework shop, A Stitch in Time, to ply their particular needlecraft, whether it be crochet, knitting, embroidery, or quilting.

At first, she had been hesitant to share details of her finds with them, all except for Alice MacFarlane, that is, who was her best friend from those summers of her youth. Gram had treated Alice like a second granddaughter, and as an adult, Alice had looked on Betsy Holden as a treasured friend and mentor. Now Alice lived down the hill in the old carriage house that had been converted years ago into living quarters and was no longer part of the same parcel of property with Grey Gables. Annie would often see her auburn-haired friend coming from and going to the various home parties she conducted for Divine Décor and Princessa Jewelry companies.

Annie and the ladies from the club had been through a few rocky patches as they got to know each other, and they had learned to trust her, as she had learned to trust them. Barring the occasional misunderstanding, they were as dear to her as her old friends back in Texas. Annie knew that if she ever decided to head south again, she would miss them terribly.

Taking a deep breath, Annie threw off the covers and rolled out of bed. After putting on her comfy bathrobe and sliding her feet into cozy slippers, she headed down the open staircase to the first floor, where she made her way toward the back of the house through the main hallway that began at the front door and ended just beyond the door to the kitchen on the right and the library on the left. She wasn't surprised to find that she was being closely followed by a small, gray, furry object. Boots, who had been her grandmother's cat, was Annie's constant companion around the house, and was especially attentive to Annie at mealtimes. After making sure that Boots's bowl was full of kibble, Annie sat down at the kitchen table to have a quick breakfast of cold cereal and milk, and an invigorating cup of coffee. She sat at that table every morning for breakfast, just as she had on those summer mornings when she stayed with Gram. Together they had enjoyed the view of the beach and the sun rising over the ocean through the kitchen window, and it pleased her to do the same now. It was a great way to start the day.

She didn't tarry long over breakfast; she had a lot to do before Wally showed up to work in the attic. Annie wanted to move as many cardboard boxes as possible to make room for him to work, and to make sure that things that were not in boxes, like furniture and old lamps, were protected from whatever mess would result from the work. She knew that she could depend on Wally to help move the heavy items. Sometimes she wondered how in the world some of the larger pieces of furniture were moved up those narrow stairs. If and when the time came to take them out of the attic, it would be helpful to know how someone had managed to get them up there in the first place!

A short time later, Annie was ready to tackle the attic, dressed in old jeans and a well-worn flannel shirt of her grandfather's that she had found in Gram's dresser and saved for just such a purpose. She tied up her shoulder–length blond hair in a red bandanna. Armed with several dust cloths, a broom and dustpan, and carrying several bed-sheets she intended to use to cover some of the larger items, she caught a glance of herself in the hallway mirror. She laughed out loud, her getup reminding her of the antics of Lucy and Ethel in an old episode of *I Love Lucy*. How Wayne would have teased her.

The thought of him made her smile. It was odd how time really did heal wounds. Her husband's death from a heart at-tack was so unexpected, and it seemed to her that the ache of his absence would never go away. But lately, she found that she was beginning to be able to think of him with less sadness, and remember instead only the love and laughter they had shared. Her time at Grey Gables had given her the distance and the distraction she needed to begin to come out of the depressed state she had been in before she left Texas.

She had felt sad and alone, or at least unneeded. She

knew that her daughter and son-in-law and grandchildren loved her, and that she had many friends who cared, but they had their own lives to live. It was a shock to think of herself as a single person in the world, when for most of her adult life she had had Wayne to confide in and to share decisions with. She felt that no other person could ever take his place, and the future had looked bleak and somewhat frightening.

Then Annie thought of Gram, and how she must have gone through the same feelings when Gramps had died. She had been happily married to Charlie Holden for over 50 years, yet after his death, she found the resolve to carry on with her career as a talented needlework designer, and remained active with her friends and in the community. Annie wished that she would've understood better what her grandmother must have been going through at that time. It was so easy to get caught up in one's own life and not fully comprehend another person's feelings. If only …

But the past couldn't be changed.

Annie opened the door and trudged up the attic stairs, feeling a bit less lighthearted than she had only moments before. She could only think that everyone must have those experiences in the past, that when they look back at how they handled certain situations, they wish they had done better. *All you can do is to try to do better the next time*, she thought.

As she entered the attic, Annie could see well enough to find the pull string of the light fixture by the faint sunlight that was filtering in through the small eyebrow windows at both ends of the attic. She had always thought that those half-oval windows gave a lot of character to the exterior of the house, and that whoever designed the house, with its many gables and unique windows, had a wonderful aesthetic sense. The original gray trim heightened the effect of the angles and highlighted special features like the eyebrow windows and the gingerbread-work around the porch.

She especially loved the porch, and back when she and Alice were young girls, they had spent many happy hours on the porch swing, talking and giggling. This was done in conjunction with other activities: Sometimes they had been given the job of snapping green beans from Gram's garden for supper that night, or they worked on crochet projects that Gram encouraged them to try. She always made sure their hands were busy.

Annie looked at her watch and realized it was after six-thirty; Wally would be there around eight o'clock. She surveyed the room, and determined a few of the larger items were fine where they were for the time being. They were mostly located along the one side of the attic, and the ones that were exposed, like the old washstand and a few high-backed chairs could just be covered with sheets. It was the center of the room under the ridge of the roof where she hoped to clear a bit. She picked up a couple of boxes, resisting the urge to look inside, and moved them toward one corner.

In the corner was a dressmaker's headless mannequin wrapped in a dusty sheet that draped to the floor; it was topped with a ghastly looking hat. Annie could never remember her grandmother wearing a hat, but she knew that all well-dressed women used to wear hats to church, at the very least, and if they were going into town to shop. How times had changed! She just hoped her grandmother had never worn that particular hat. Annie peeked through a small gap in the sheet and discovered that there was some sort of garment underneath. If the hat had anything to do with it, it probably wasn't worth bothering with.

At the present, it was just in her way. Considering the number of things she needed to move, she decided that it could be taken down to one of the empty bedrooms. At least the boxes could be stacked to take up less space. She lifted off the hat, looked inside to determine that there were no spiderwebs, and perched it on top of her head. She thought to herself, *I must really look ridiculous now!* She managed to wrap her left arm around the waist and carefully lifted the mannequin from its spot. Then she negotiated it through the narrow, somewhat winding path among the contents of the attic to the stairs. She decided it would be best to back down the stairs to avoid getting tripped up in the trailing sheet. Hanging on to the banister with her right hand, she slowly made her way down to the second floor of Grey Gables. She was relieved when she successfully delivered the mannequin and the hat to one of the extra bedrooms.

Annie lightly climbed back up the attic stairs, encouraged by the little bit of progress she was making. Returning to the corner where the mannequin had stood, she saw a round box topped with a matching-size piece of cardboard in the place where the mannequin had been standing. She hadn't noticed the box before since the sheet on the mannequin had hidden it. She removed the cardboard to uncover a beautifully decorated hatbox.

Someone had painted a mixed bouquet of flowers, tied together with ribbon and lace, on the top of the lid with a wreath of ivy around the edges; Annie recognized a couple of the varieties in the bouquet from her walks in the woods and fields above the shoreline. Gram made sure that Annie learned the name of each kind of wildflower, and she had never forgotten those lessons. Some were common garden flowers; there was only one type of flower she couldn't place.

She wondered if that awful hat she had just worn downstairs had been carried home in that beautiful box. *That would be ironic, ... or would that be incongruous? ... or just a disagreeable coincidence? ... Whatever ... it just seems wrong.* She had an overwhelming desire to look inside the box. She told herself it was probably empty. Picking up the hatbox, she decided to take it to the bedroom to reunite it with the mannequin. She'd get to it later.

Annie spent the next hour or so working in the attic until she heard the faint sound of the doorbell below. She had made some good progress, and she thought there was enough room for Wally to get started. After they exchanged greetings, Wally followed Annie up to the attic as she explained what she had done that morning. He seemed to think he could manage for the time being on his own, so she left him to his work. He would be carrying in tools and the electrical supplies needed, along with some battery-powered lights since the electricity would have to be turned off in that part of the house; he would have to run an extension cord from other parts of the house to power his tools.

Annie planned to stay out of his way. Since it was

Tuesday, she thought she'd run some errands downtown before heading to A Stitch in Time for the weekly meeting of the Hook and Needle Club. Feeling hot and grimy after her workout in the attic, she took a quick shower and dressed casually in gray slacks and a light blue blouse.

Thinking about what she needed to do before she left the house, she noticed she had left the door ajar to the bedroom where she had deposited the mannequin and the hatbox. Since Annie returned to Grey Gables, she had taken to sleeping in her grandmother's old bedroom for a couple of reasons: She felt comforted being in the room where her grandmother had slept, and it had the best view of the ocean. There were three other bedrooms on the second floor; one had been her mother's childhood room, and another had been Annie's during the summers. The "visitor's bedroom," as her grandmother had named it, was where she placed the mannequin. She automatically went to close the door, but had a second thought.

"I'd better make sure I don't shut Boots in there," she said out loud.

It had happened before that she had unintentionally shut Boots in; she didn't want to do that again. It made for one unhappy cat. She checked between the pillows on the bed and under it. It was possible that Boots had scooted out the front door when Wally arrived. It was hard to keep up with her sometimes.

Annie was about to leave the room when the mannequin caught her eye. She had plenty of time before the club meeting would begin, and she didn't have that many errands to take care of. Why not see what the garment looked like now? How bad could it be? She could take a closer look at the hatbox too.

She had placed the hat back on the top of the manne-quin, but she moved it now to the top of the dresser. She looked to see how the sheet was attached; it was wrapped around the figure like a Greek chiton, only with a flap over the top of the neck. It was held together with a few strategically placed safety pins. Annie started undoing the lower pins, working her way up, so that she could remove the sheet with one dramatic flourish. When she was sure no other pins remained, she undid the final one, and grabbing a corner of the sheet, gave it a tug. Intending to say "Tah-dah!" she was stopped in mid "Tah" by what she saw.

Annie had uncovered a beautiful and elegant dress. It was obviously from a time before her grandmother's; it looked like something Annie imagined a Gibson girl from the turn of the last century might have worn. Though the formerly white fabric had yellowed to a soft ivory with age, Annie could see that it must have been expensive and was still very lovely. The dress had a high collar, puffy sleeves with long cuffs, a very narrow waist, and a wide ruffle around the bottom hem. Covering the cuffs and the collar, extend-ing over the shoulders ending in a V shape on the front and back of the bodice were the most beautiful pieces of hand-crocheted threadwork she had ever seen. Each piece was delicately made, and the thread shimmered in the light. Annie thought it might be silk, but she was used to working with yarn more often than thread, so she wasn't sure.

Annie turned to the hatbox. After taking another admiring glance at the painting on the lid, she removed it, and gasped with delight at what she saw inside. From the box she carefully lifted a hand-crocheted wedding veil that appeared to be about waist length, and a pair of crocheted gloves, all clearly fashioned with the same fine hand that had worked the pieces of crochet that were sewn to the dress. Annie laid the ivory veil across the dark-color bedcover to have a better look. The top portion of the veil was tightly gathered and attached to the back of a flexible wire circle that was covered with meticulously crocheted mint green leaves and tiny pale pink flowers. Where the lower part of the veil flared out, Annie could see scattered images of flowers and birds. It was a picture made in crochet.

Annie had seen filet crochet pieces before. She always marveled at the way scores of filled-in blocks and open spaces were positioned to make intricate pictures and sometimes words. She had never tried to make anything like that herself. Her first attempt at crocheting with thread was the set of curtains that were now hanging in her grandmother's bedroom. She had used size 10 cotton thread and a size 6 steel hook. The curtains had taken weeks to make, and she was pleased with the results. But as she looked at the workmanship on the dress, the veil, and the gloves, she was aware that the woman who had made these articles was more than a casual needleworker—she was an artist.

Annie considered the dress again. Obviously, it was meant to be a wedding dress. She knew it hadn't been her grandmother's; that was in a box in the bedroom closet. She'd found it there when she was going through her grandmother's personal belongings after she arrived in Stony Point following Gram's death. A picture of Gram and Gramps on their wedding day was on the mantel in the living room. Besides, this dress appeared to be from a completely different era.

Annie gently arranged the slight train at the back of the dress so that she could get a complete picture of the dress, the veil, and the gloves. In her mind's eye, she formed an image of a woman in the dress, with alabaster skin and dark upswept hair encircled by the pink-flowered garland, the veil draped down her back. In her tiny gloved hands she held the same bouquet of flowers that was illustrated on the lid of the hatbox. Annie imagined her as she walked down the aisle beside her father, a distinguished, bearded, older man in a navy blue suit ...

Suddenly, Annie came out of her reverie and realized that time had been passing quickly while she was imagining how the dress might have looked when it was worn—or had it been worn at all? The wedding ensemble presented Annie with many questions: Why did Gram hide it away in the attic? Did the crocheter make the gown for herself, or for someone else? Who was she? Looking at her watch, Annie realized she'd have to save all her questions for later. She'd better get going if she was going to get to the meeting on time. She was looking forward to sharing what she had found with everyone at the Hook and Needle Club.

~ 2 ~

nnie entered A Stitch in Time through the frosted-glass front door, feeling as she always did, that she had entered needlecrafters' heaven. The sight of soft, richly colored yarn combined with a wall display of pattern books seemed to call her to browse and to purchase new yarns and patterns, even though at present she was already working on a couple of projects: a close-fitting cloche with a matching "lapghan" from cotton yarn for a friend back in Texas who would soon be undergoing chemotherapy, and a soft green-and-yellow baby blanket to donate to a local organization that provided supplies to expectant mothers who needed help. Normally, she only liked to work on one project at a time, but lately there seemed to be several needs that she wanted to help fill with comforting gifts. Thinking of that, it was sometimes hard to resist the pull of acquiring new yarn for a future project.

But she did resist for the time being, directing her attention to the circle of comfy chairs where the ladies of the Hook and Needle Club were already gathered. By the time Annie had gotten out of the door at Grey Gables, and stopped at the post office and bank, she was several minutes behind schedule.

Mary Beth Brock, the owner of the shop, was standing by the polished-wood counter and greeted Annie warmly.

After Annie's longtime friend Alice, Mary Beth was one of the first people to really make Annie feel welcome in Stony Point. Not only did she invite Annie to join the Hook and Needle Club, but she proved to be a good friend through several rough patches with some of the other ladies when Annie was a newcomer.

Annie took her place among the circle of ladies, looking at the faces of her friends. Alice was there, concentrating on embroidering a floral tea-towel edging. Alice had always admired Annie's grandmother's cross-stitch creations and had never really taken to crochet the way that Annie had, so it was natural that she gravitated to the needlecraft practiced by the woman who had always been so kind to her.

Kate Stevens, who worked for Mary Beth in the shop, was taking advantage of a momentary lull of customers, sitting at the edge of the circle working on her own design—a high-waisted, orchid-color crocheted top with short sleeves. When finished, the design would be displayed in the store for all to admire. Kate's talent for design was becoming quite well-known among customers who liked to crochet and wanted her patterns, and among others who just wanted to purchase Kate's finished pieces.

Peggy Carson, wife of handyman Wally, was appliqué-ing pink and lavender fabric pieces onto a cream-color fabric square. Annie knew that the pieces would fit together to form the image of a ballerina; Peggy's little daughter, Emily, had dreams of being a dancer when she grew up and loved having her mother's quilted blankets, pillow covers, and wall hangings to decorate her room.

As usual, Stella Brickson, the oldest member of the

group, sat ramrod straight in her chair as her knitting
needles clicked rhythmically, pausing only occasionally
when she gave her variegated blue and green yarn a yank as
she added another row to her afghan. Her silver-gray hair
should have softened her appearance, but Stella's severe-
style choice only served to emphasize her air of no-nonsense.

The final member, Gwendolyn Palmer, seemed especially vibrant that day. She looked immaculate, as she
always did—her blond hair perfectly styled, her classic-style
clothing perfectly neat with never a wrinkle, and of course,
her matching accessories—earrings, necklace, bracelet, and
silk neck scarf—completed her look. Though Annie could
dress up with the best of them, Gwen's everyday ensembles
sometimes made Annie feel like her outfits represented the
"don't" picture in a fashion magazine.

Looking up from the beautiful gold/green/purple Fair
Isle pillow cover that she was knitting, Gwen said, "Oh,
Annie, I was waiting for you to come. I have some great
news to share with everyone. Our youngest son, Tony, is
coming home for a visit." Looking at Annie, she said, "I
don't think you have met him yet. He just finished his MBA
at Harvard and has been touring the British Isles for the last
month. Since he's been in college and working part-time, he
hasn't had the opportunity to come home very often—just
at Christmas usually—but he called on Sunday to say that
he was heading back to the States and would be stopping
in Stony Point for a while. He said he's bringing home a
surprise for me. I just can't wait to see him! We're so proud,
of course. There was some talk that he might join his father
at the bank, but he's had offers in Boston and New York, so

I guess it's probably too much to hope that he might settle here. Still …"

Gwen's face was just radiant as she continued to talk about her son. Annie didn't think she had ever seen Gwen so animated. Gwendolyn and John Palmer were among what might be called the "upstanding citizens" of the town. He was president of Stony Point Bank, and both of them were involved in numerous community organizations. Their home was a reflection of everything else in their lives—it was perfectly kept, in the midst of a well-manicured lawn and formal flower garden. In fact, the Palmer house was located just around the hill from Grey Gables on Ocean Drive. When Annie first saw their home from the outside, she thought how shabby it made Grey Gables appear. It made her all the more determined to return Grey Gables to its former glory.

Gwen continued, "Next Saturday afternoon, about two, we're planning to have a few friends and family over to the house to welcome him home and to celebrate him getting his degree, and I would love it if all of you could come. Please don't bring gifts; we just want to have a nice get-together. Cards are fine; they make a nice remembrance of the day. I hope Wally will be able to come too," she said, looking at Peggy, who was the only other one of the group with a husband, "and Emily too. Tony's flight will be coming into Boston on Thursday, and he's planning to drive up to Stony Point on Saturday morning."

"I'll have to check with Wally, but I think we're free to come," Peggy said. "So, you have no idea what your surprise might be?" Peggy was always on the lookout for the latest news she could share over at the Main Street diner, The Cup & Saucer, where she worked as a waitress. "It could be something really cool like I've seen on that TV shopping show; they always have such beautiful woven items—wool shawls and throws from Scotland, or table linens from Ireland—those are gorgeous. Or he might even bring you an English porcelain tea set!"

"I'm sure that whatever it is, it will be wonderful. All I really care about is to have him home for a while. I love all of my children, but I think the youngest is the hardest to let go. Even though he's an adult and has been out of the house for a long time, I still sometimes think of him as my little boy." Gwen stopped for a moment, slightly embarrassed that she had made that admission.

Stella made a sound that resembled "Harrumph!" Annie inwardly said, *Oh no*—she was sure they were all about to hear one of Stella's tirades. It wasn't that Stella meant to step on toes; she just didn't seem to even realize that she might bruise someone's feelings with her "frankness." Annie had been the recipient of Stella's direct words more than once, and sometimes it had been hurtful, but nevertheless, she understood, as did the others, that it was just Stella's "way," and that underneath it all she really had a good heart.

"That's the problem with young people these days," Stella began. "They remain children for far too long. When my husband finished college, he didn't go off dilly-dallying on some extended vacation. He went right to work, and worked every day, except Sundays of course, for the next fifty years. That's what it means to be an adult. Tony needs to stop running around and settle down and get to work. He can't always expect you and John to take care of him."

"We don't 'take care of him,'" Gwen sniffed. "Certainly, we have helped him as we have helped all of our children get started. He has worked long and hard to complete his graduate degree, including working part-time during the school year and as an intern over the summers. He deserves a break, and if we can afford to provide that for him, I don't see anything wrong with that."

"Of course there isn't," said Mary Beth, hoping to soothe Gwen's ruffled feathers and change the direction of the conversation. "I'm sure that making the choice of where to work and settle down has been on Tony's mind all the time. It's a big decision to make. It would be great to have him here in Stony Point. I saw him last year just before Christmas when he came in the shop to find a special present for you. He's such a nice young man, and so handsome—he would really be a great catch for some lucky girl. Does he have a girlfriend?"

"He's had a few girlfriends over the years, but there's no one special right now," replied Gwen. "For a while we thought that he and Shelby Spencer, his high school sweetheart, would get married, but a couple of years after he went away to college, they broke up. He dated several girls after that, but I don't think there was ever anyone he was really serious about. He has time now to find the right person."

Alice spoke without looking up from her tea towel, "Better to find the 'right' person—speaking from experience." Alice had been through a divorce, and had only recently been willing to even mention anything relating to it. Annie thought that time had begun to heal Alice's heart, as it had her own. Though the widow and the divorcée have different experiences, Annie had come to realize that in many ways they share the same conditions of sadness, loneliness, and uncertainty. She and Alice had been able to console and support each other, and it had made their friendship stronger.

Kate put down her crochet for a moment and said, "I'm trying to teach Vanessa that it's best to make sure that the person you fall in love with and marry is really someone with the same outlook and commitment to a long-term relationship, but sometimes it's so hard to get through that 'know-that-already' attitude that teenagers seem to have. I guess I was the same way. You just want your children to learn from your mistakes." Kate's marriage was another casualty of divorce, and she wanted so much to shield her teenage daughter from the hurt she had experienced.

"Well, it's not something I have to worry about with Tony right now," said Gwen. "I know he's focused on his career, and when the time comes he'll find someone who's worthy of him." Gwen cringed at her own words and then smiled. "That didn't come out just right—you know what I mean. He really is a wonderful young man, and I'm not just saying that because I'm his mother. I'm sure that the woman who becomes his wife will be someone appropriate—as you said, Kate, with the same outlook and long-term commitment to their marriage. I just want to see my children be happy."

"A worthy cause!" said Mary Beth laughing. The bell on the shop's door rang as it opened, and two ladies entered, making a beeline to the wall of pattern books. They were obviously regular customers. Mary Beth looked over at Kate and said, "I'll get this."

Annie took the opportunity in the break of the discussion about Tony Palmer to broach the topic of the wedding dress she had found in the attic that morning. "Speaking of marriage, guess what I found in Gram's attic this morning."

"Prince Charming?" guessed Alice, smiling slyly. "I always knew there was some reason you spend so much time in that attic."

The other ladies laughed, except for Stella, who didn't seem to think it was all that amusing. Peggy laid down her needle and fabric, and said, "Do we have another mystery to solve? I was just saying to Wally this morning that it was about time for you to find something new for us to work on. Come on … tell us! What did you find?"

"Well, you know that Wally came over this morning to improve the lighting situation in the attic, so I went up there early to try to make some space for him to work. There was an old dressmaker's mannequin that was in the way …"

"I remember that," Alice said, "It was there when we were kids—back in the far corner. Dusty old thing. Can't imagine a mystery connected with that."

Annie responded, "I don't remember there being a mannequin in the attic back then … I guess it just didn't make an impact on me. Do you remember the wedding dress?"

"Wedding dress? No, it was just plain, with nothing on it," Alice answered.

"Well, there is something on it now. The whole thing was covered with an old sheet, and I carried it down to the extra bedroom this morning, along with a really ugly old hat that was perched on top. Oh, and I found that there was a beautiful hand-painted hatbox sitting underneath it—I took that downstairs too."

Kate spoke dreamily, "I just love old hatboxes. And I love hats. I should have been born back in those days when ladies wore long dresses and hats and gloves, and sipped mint juleps as they waved their silk fans on the veranda during the long, hot summer."

"I think we're getting off topic here," said Peggy, giving Kate a sideways glance, with a hint of a sardonic smile. "What about this wedding dress?"

"I knew that there was some sort of garment under the sheet, 'cause I peeked. I carried the mannequin down to the visitor's bedroom to get it out of the way. It was only after I removed the sheet that covered it, and saw the contents of the hatbox, that I knew for sure it had been someone's wedding dress. Because of the awful hat that had been sitting on it, I was expecting the dress to be something really garish, so I was completely surprised when it turned out to be so gorgeous. It reminds me of a Gibson-girl dress, but the really outstanding part is the hand-crocheted accents on the cuffs, collar and bodice. The dress is obviously old; it's a rich ivory color."

"Could it have been Betsy's wedding dress?" asked Gwen.

"No, I found Gram's wedding dress ages ago—folded and put away in a box in her closet," Annie explained. "This dress doesn't really look like it's from Gram's era at all. It looks like it might be from the turn of the last century. But I haven't told you what I found in the hatbox yet."

Annie looked around at the faces of her friends.

Mary Beth had finished with her customers and had been listening in. Peggy's eyes had widened as she listened with expectation to learn about the contents of the hatbox. Everyone had their eyes on Annie, except Stella, who never dropped a stitch as her knitting needles continued to click together. Annie wasn't fooled though; she'd been around Stella long enough to know that she never missed a thing, even when she pretended she wasn't listening.

"First of all, the hatbox is decorated with a beautiful painting of a bouquet of flowers. So anyway, I opened the box, and there was a hand-crocheted veil and pair of gloves that match the crocheted pieces on the dress. You won't believe how elegant it looks. I can't imagine to whom it might have belonged, or why it was in Gram's attic—especially since it wasn't on the mannequin when we were kids. That's kind of strange."

"Well, if Betsy put the dress on the mannequin, maybe she bought it at a sale or something, just to preserve the handwork on the dress," suggested Alice.

"I guess that's possible," replied Annie, "but why 'save' something just to hide it away in the attic like that?"

"If it's as old as you think it is, have you considered that it might have belonged to the previous owner of Grey Gables?" asked Stella.

"Well, no," said Annie, slightly startled that Stella would actually offer an idea about the origin of the dress. "I don't even know who that was. Why would they have left something so personal in the house?"

Ignoring Annie's question, Stella said, "Didn't your grandmother ever tell you about Captain Grey? Charlie and Betsy bought Grey Gables after he died, though I don't suppose that either of them knew him very well. Nobody did really. He lived alone and kept to himself most of the time. He had a housekeeper who fixed his meals and cleaned, but I don't think he went out much in those last years. I only saw him once or twice myself."

"The house was named after a person? I always thought it was called that because of all of the gray-color accents on the exterior of the house. I don't recall that the subject of the previous owner ever came up with Gram. Besides, why would an old bachelor sea captain have a wedding dress?" asked Annie.

~3~

nnie was still thinking about Captain Grey as she left A Stitch in Time. It was rather exciting to think that Grey Gables was named after a sea captain. She wondered why Gram had never mentioned him, but then, since Annie had returned to Stony Point, she had found that there was a lot more to her grandmother's life than she had previously known. It probably shouldn't have surprised her when she came across another detail that she hadn't been aware of before.

Annie headed next door to The Cup & Saucer, where the locals sometimes stopped for a bite of something to eat and perhaps to hear the latest news and/or gossip of the area. Often she and Alice would have lunch together after the meeting, but today Alice had a Divine Décor home party to attend and had to bow out. Annie didn't mind. When she first arrived in Stony Point, she felt like everyone in the diner was staring at her, but now she was like another one of the locals. It had taken some time, but she really felt that she had been accepted as part of the community, even if she was "from away."

As she opened the door to enter the diner, Ian Butler, the town's mayor, was just exiting. Since it was a work day, Ian wore his typical button-down shirt and tie, but today he had also added a casual suit jacket. Annie involuntarily thought how handsome he looked; Ian's eyes lit up and a smile spontaneously spread across his face when he saw Annie. It was no secret in town that Ian, who had been widowed about the same time as Annie, had a soft spot for her. Though Annie told herself that he was "just a friend," she couldn't help but notice that her pulse seemed to quicken when he was near.

"Annie! I was just looking for you. I was hoping that you'd be stopping by here today after the Hook and Needle meeting. If you don't have previous plans, would you care to have lunch with me and someone that I'm meeting over at the Maplehurst Inn restaurant? I only ask because it concerns Grey Gables."

"How so?" asked Annie.

"I had a call this morning from an artist named Andrew Gareth. He has plans to do a series of paintings of different sites around Stony Point, and Grey Gables is one of the places he wants to include. I suggested that I meet with him to discuss his project over lunch at the inn, since that's where he's staying. Then, after I hung up, I thought I'd invite you as well—hoping you'd be available. I'm sure he won't mind if I show up with a lovely companion who has a vested interest," Ian answered, smiling.

As Annie listened to Ian, her eyes had grown wide. "Andrew Gareth? The artist Andrew Gareth? Wow! He's here? Now? And Stony Point is going to be his next subject? That is so amazing!"

Ian's face took on a bemused aspect. "So, it appears you've heard of this guy."

"Heard of him? Well, yes! He's an incredibly talented

artist. I saw a program about him on public TV a long time ago, and when he had an exhibition in Texas a couple of years ago, Wayne and I went to see it. It was just so interesting, and his paintings are breathtaking. I can't believe he's here; though, now that I think about it, Stony Point is right up his alley. This is so exciting!"

"I think we've established that you're impressed," Ian said with an air of ambivalence. "What else do you know about him?"

"Well—just what I learned from the television program, and the brochure from the art exhibit, really. It's so fascinating how he works. When he started as a young artist, he hit on the idea of traveling to each state in the Union and finding a small town that he felt was representative of that state's "personality." After studying the locale he's chosen— its landscape, its architecture, and even, to a certain extent, the history of the town and its citizens—he works up a series of paintings that shows significant images from the area and from the town's past, including people, buildings, landmarks, et cetera. He avoids the bigger and better-known towns, saying that the small towns experience less change, and the people there still carry the flavor of the original settlers. He has a knack for communicating the character of a place and of the people who live there. I don't know how he does it, but when you go to one of his exhibitions, you come away with an abiding impression that you've been introduced to an old friend. ... That doesn't make any sense does it? It's like when you meet someone for the first time, but somehow you feel like you've known them your whole life."

Looking at Annie intently, Ian said, "It does make

sense—I know exactly what you mean." He paused for a moment before continuing. "Then I guess you're in for lunch with us today?"

"Absolutely! Thanks so much for including me. You said he wants to paint a portrait of Grey Gables? That would be so wonderful. I think Gram would have liked to know that her home was being immortalized by a famous painter."

"From what you've said, I take it that you've never met Mr. Gareth in person."

"No, I've only seen him on that television program—and that was maybe ten years ago. The Texas exhibition was traveling all over the state—Austin, Dallas, Houston—it's a big state. Anyway, I believe that Mr. Gareth had already moved on to begin his next project at that time. I guess between the time it takes to find the town he wants to focus on, and then the research, and choosing what he will be painting, and then the painting itself—I recall him saying on the program that it takes more than a year for each state. It really is the work of a lifetime."

"It seems fortunate that he chose Grey Gables as his subject; since you are already familiar with his work, I'm sure it will make his job here easier," said Ian, with an "after-you" flourish of his hand.

Annie and Ian began walking the short distance along Main Street, with its old-fashioned lampposts and coastal-town ambiance, to Maplehurst Inn, a charming colonial-style hotel with an adjoining restaurant where out-of-towners and locals went for a more formal dining experience than was to be found at The Cup & Saucer.

Annie fell silent, and Ian seemed to sense that she didn't

want to engage in conversation as they walked. In fact, in her mind she was reliving the day that she and Wayne had made the short journey into Dallas to see Andrew Gareth's paintings. They didn't often get to take extended vacations with the demands of their business, but they tried to get away on day or weekend trips, now and then, to take advantage of cultural events, like concerts and art shows, and to see some of the historical sites that preserved the rich history of Texas. One of the things that made the Gareth exhibition so interesting was the way it combined art and history. It had been such a wonderful outing. She had told Ian that it was "a couple of years ago," but now she realized that it was also the last day trip she and Wayne had taken before his death. Only that morning, she had thought that she'd learned how to cope with her feelings of loss, but the familiar pain of his absence came to her again, and tears began to pool in the corners of her eyes.

By then, she and Ian had reached the Inn. Ian opened the glass door and followed Annie into the spacious foyer. The hotel's front desk was situated at one end and the entry to the restaurant at the other. In the transition from bright sunlight to the soft lighting of the entry, Annie was able to brush away a stray tear that had fallen down her cheek. She hoped that Ian didn't notice, and she blinked several times to clear the remainder of the tears from her eyes. Taking a deep breath, she determined she would put aside those memories for the time being; it was best to revisit them only when she was alone.

As her eyes adjusted to the dimmer light, Annie glanced around the inn's elegantly decorated restaurant to see if she could recognize the famous painter. She had only seen his image on television and on the brochure she had picked up at the exhibition in Texas. The dining room was packed—it was the height of the tourist season, and local hotels were fully booked; from the looks of things, restaurants were seeing business boom as well. With so many people, Annie doubted that she would be able to pick out Mr. Gareth.

She was saved the effort when the hostess approached them. "Mr. Mayor! It's nice to see you here again. Mr. Gareth is already seated—he told me that he'd be meeting with 'Mr. Butler.' I assumed it must be you—I don't often see your brother Todd in here in the middle of a weekday. Hi Annie! Will you be joining them?"

Annie nodded, and Ian said, "Hi Kellie—nice to see you too. Yes, Annie's joining us today. Hope there's room. Glad to see that the restaurant is doing well."

Kellie answered, "No worries; I seated him at a table for four. I know how you are about bringing along 'extras.' And yes, business has been great. It seems like we have more tourists every season. They must have heard about our hunky mayor and want to have a look for themselves," she said with a mischievous grin. "If you'll just follow me, now, I'll lead you to Mr. Gareth."

Picking up a couple of menus on her way, Kellie led Annie and Ian to a table across the room, where there was seated a darkly attractive, middle-aged man with wavy black hair, and a short, rather scruffy beard streaked with high-lights of gray. As Andrew Gareth rose to greet them, the smile that appeared on his lips carried through to his dark brown eyes, but the expression on his face was nevertheless distant, as if he was in another world. He was tall and angular, and to Annie he looked as though he had just stepped out of a painting by El Greco.

"Mayor Butler, I presume," said Andrew, offering his hand to Ian. Turning to Annie, he said, "And do I have the pleasure of meeting Mrs. Butler?"

Ian smiled; Annie blushed and replied, "No, Mr. Gareth, I'm Annie Dawson. I own Grey Gables, and Ian tells me that you would like to make a painting of my home."

"Yes! That's right. It's a wonderful house from the Victorian era, and there is such an interesting history surrounding the original owner, Zacharias Grey," said Andrew.

"Do you mean Captain Grey?" asked Annie.

"Yes. Captain Zacharias Grey. He had a long career as a merchant seaman. I have a particular interest in his life. He accomplished a great deal, but there was so much sadness too."

Annie said, "It's quite a coincidence, hearing that name for the second time today when I only just heard of Captain Grey for the very first time this morning. I'd be very interested to learn what you know about him, and about the history of Grey Gables before my grandparents bought the house, Mr. Gareth."

"Please call me Andrew, and I hope I may call you Ian and Annie. Let's all have a seat." As he pulled out a chair for Annie, he said, "At present, I'd really just like to talk about the locations I'm considering as subjects for my Maine exhibition. The knowledge that longtime local residents have to impart is often as valuable to me as the information I find in libraries and at historical societies."

After taking his own seat, Andrew turned to Annie and said, "I hope we will have some time in the future to discuss Captain Grey."

Annie tried to hide her disappointment. Thinking about it, she imagined that it wasn't his habit to discuss all of the details of his research while he was working on a project. "I look forward to that discussion Mr. ... I mean, Andrew. I'm afraid I won't be much help as a 'longtime resident'—I only moved into Grey Gables after my grandmother died. But if there's anything you need to know about Stony Point, our mayor is the man to see."

Ian smiled, but modestly brushed aside the compliment. Speaking to Andrew he said, "I appreciate your call to let us know that you'll be working in the area."

"Actually, I've been around for a while, doing some research and checking out the locality. I've rented some space on Main Street—over the store Dress to Impress—for a studio. I hope that I can trust in you both to keep my purpose here to yourselves as much as possible. I'm not what you'd call a celebrity, but nevertheless, it has happened that certain 'fans'—for want of a better word—have been known to follow me about if they know where I am, and I'd really like to avoid that. I need solitude when I'm painting, for the most part, and the fewer distractions, the better," said Andrew. "I like to inform the powers that be—usually the mayor, or the head of the town council—about what I'm doing, in case any questions arise. And of course, I have to inform the owners of private property when I want to make a painting of a house like yours, Annie."

"What other places are you looking at as possible

subjects?" Ian asked.

"Besides Grey Gables ... I want to include Butler's Lighthouse and the fisherman's harbor; also the Town Square and the library, of course—it's an outstanding example of the Greek-Revival style that was popular from the late eighteenth to the mid-nineteenth century, and it says a great deal about the early citizens of Stony Point, and of Maine itself."

"What do you mean?" asked Annie.

"The architecture of a place is about more than just providing shelter and being pleasant to look at; both private and public buildings, and the surrounding spaces, tell us about the character of the people who built them and of the people who have lived and worked in them since, by what they have seen fit to preserve. When the town of Stony Point was being formed, shipbuilding and shipping was a major part of that growth—that was the case throughout Maine, for that matter. The seafaring life was hard, but it gave men a chance to see the world. They had an opportunity to see how others lived, and it made them conscious of better ways—and worse. Naturally, a better way of life was something they wanted to provide for their families. They thought about their progeny in the distant future too—they wanted to leave something that would endure for those generations that were yet to come. If you know what to look for, you can almost read the minds of those from the past in public buildings, and the private ones as well. Grey Gables, for instance, shows that the architect, the builder, the owner, all wanted to make something that was more than just pleasing to the eye. I sense that there was an effort to express their knowledge of the world beyond the confines of a small, if you'll forgive me, Mayor, backwater town, and their hopes for a grander future."

"That's quite all right," Ian said. "Stony Point has come a long way since the early days in many respects, but speaking as a lifetime resident and mayor, our goal has never been about growth for growth's sake, or to achieve any kind of 'grandeur.' We're interested in maintaining a way of life for our citizens that includes opportunities—good jobs and good schools—and a sense of community that provides a safe and accepting atmosphere where families and individuals can put down roots. It's not just a place to live; it's home."

"Spoken like a true politician ... and a good man who loves his community," said Andrew tactfully. "It was not my intention to denigrate Stony Point. I love small towns. That's one of the reasons I've made capturing them on canvas my life's work. I'm actually saying the same thing as you are—that the people responsible for building structures like the library and Grey Gables had the same hopes for the residents of Stony Point as you have just described, though newcomers may have had a more difficult time fitting in to the established structure back then."

There's still some of that resistance to newcomers, thought Annie, remembering some of her first experiences in Stony Point when she was new in town after Gram's death—and she was not even a complete outsider, as the granddaughter of Charlie and Betsy Holden. She was so thankful for the friendship with Alice in her first few weeks in Stony Point. She might have just given up and gone back to Texas. *No,* she contradicted herself, *I wouldn't have; it's not in my nature.*

Andrew continued, "But I think there was an expectation, at least by some of the early leaders, that Stony Point could one day rival Boston and Portland. They invested time and treasure in city planning that resulted in the charm that draws tourists here today. There are many small towns along the coast, but most people agree that Stony Point offers something special, and it keeps them coming back year after year."

Ian agreed, "That's one of the things that visitors often tell us—that Stony Point is 'charming' and makes them feel like they've returned to a more gracious time."

With that comment, the waitress came to their table to take their orders. Ian and Andrew continued to talk about the various locations that Andrew was interested in painting, and Ian offered many insights into the history of Stony Point. It had been his family who were responsible for the construction of the lighthouse that bore their name, and he offered to introduce Andrew to his brother, Todd, who had a fleet of lobster boats and knew a lot about the history of the harbor.

Annie listened to the two men with interest. She knew that Ian was a fount of knowledge about all things concerning Stony Point, but she was impressed by his ability to converse with such ease with Andrew Gareth, whose experience of the world-at-large would appear to be greater than Ian's, about aspects of art and history in a much wider context than the local scene. She had to admit: The more she learned about Ian Butler, the more she liked him.

The three ate their meal in a leisurely fashion, coupled with intense conversation not only about Stony Point, but also about Andrew's previous work, and why he felt it was important to try to capture the essential individuality of each state on canvas. By the time they had finished with their desserts, the restaurant was considerably less crowded.

Even Ian seemed surprised at how quickly the time had flown. Glancing at his watch, he said, "How did it get to be two o'clock? I'm sorry to break this off, but I have a council meeting this afternoon." Ian stood and extended his hand to Andrew. "It's been a pleasure meeting you Andrew, and I look forward to more discussions while you're here in Stony Point. Be sure to let me know if there is anything I can do to help you with your project." He turned to Annie and said, "Thanks so much for joining us, Annie. May I see you to your car?"

"No thanks, Ian," Annie replied, "I have a couple more errands to take care of in town before I head back to Grey Gables. Thanks for inviting me. I've learned a lot today, listening to the both of you. It's been really interesting."

Looking at Annie, Andrew said, "Shall we arrange to meet to discuss the portrait of Grey Gables?"

"Certainly … ," Annie replied. "Would next Monday work for you? It should be calm and quiet at Grey Gables— I don't have any plans for the day, and it's unlikely that anything will disturb us."

"Monday it is then. I'll give you a call later in the week, and we can set a specific time. I'd like to do a few sketches of the exterior to try to find the best aspect for the painting. I'm really looking forward to seeing the interior of Grey Gables too."

4

The following Saturday morning found Annie, a basket in hand, standing in the attic of Grey Gables surveying the work that Wally had completed. Annie had gone the practical route, choosing two lengths of track lighting that Wally had installed along the underside of the ridge of the roof. Now she could flip a switch from beside the door instead of struggling to make her way to the center of the room to pull a string for the single bare lightbulb that used to hang there. The new lighting wasn't exactly what Annie would have called attractive, but it accomplished what she had wanted; the directional lamps lit all the corners of the attic.

However, rather than encouraging her, at the moment it only seemed to magnify the enormity of her never-ending task: sorting through the detritus of her grandmother's attic. It seemed like the extra light had magically multiplied the number of boxes and containers. She noticed more dust and cobwebs. She began to wonder, *Am I ever going to be able to finish this?*

Looking at her watch, she knew she couldn't just stand there all day. *How did it get to be ten o'clock?* She normally spent Saturday mornings getting caught up on cleaning jobs around the rest of the house, a habit she'd acquired when she was working full-time at the car dealership in Texas. This had taken on an added urgency since Andrew was coming over on Monday. She wanted to show Grey Gables at its best, or its best possible at the time being.

She'd already gotten behind schedule because of a phone call from a friend in Texas. It was great to catch up on the news in Brookfield, but they'd talked for over an hour. Afterward, she'd come up to the attic to see if she could find a basket she could use to store some new skeins of yarn that she had bought at A Stitch in Time on Friday. She accomplished her mission, but then she had gotten sidetracked as she looked over the attic with its new, brighter aspect.

She switched off the lights and headed back down the attic stairs, ticking off the list of things she wanted to get done before lunchtime: the kitchen and mudroom floors needed to be washed; the library seriously needed dusting, and the living room carpet swept; there was that pile of ironing she'd been putting off ... and she'd have to make sure she had enough time to shower and change before two o'clock, the time when Tony Palmers' homecoming party was planned to begin.

Annie was halfway down the main staircase, noticing that the dark wooden balusters that held up the banister could use a good polish too, when the telephone in the living room began to ring. Picking up her pace, Annie was breathing slightly heavier when she got to the phone. She was surprised to hear Gwendolyn Palmers' voice on the line.

"Annie? Could you come over to Wedgwood right away? I'm afraid I need your help."

"Of course, Gwen—is everything all right?" asked Annie.

"Yes, we're all right ... it's just ... I mean, there's just been an unexpected development, and … I'll explain when you get here. Please just come as soon as you can." And with that Gwen hung up the phone.

Annie stood for only a moment looking at the receiver in her hand. *How very odd*, she thought. It wasn't like Gwen to be so cryptic. Immediately, Annie went to get her purse and keys from the side table in the entry hall. She glanced in the oval mirror that hung above the table. She'd barely combed her hair that morning, and she wasn't wearing any makeup. *Au naturel it is*, she thought as she ran her fingers through her hair in an attempt to tidy it. *Guess it goes with the jeans and T-shirt look.*

The Palmers' home, called Wedgwood, was just around the hill from Grey Gables on Ocean Drive, and between the time it took Annie to walk out the door, get in her car, start it, and drive to the Palmers' house, it took less than ten minutes to arrive. In fact, Annie and Alice planned to walk over together to the Palmers' for the party that afternoon. But Gwendolyn had sounded so strange on the phone; Annie wanted to get there as quickly as she could.

Annie pulled her classic Malibu into the Palmers' driveway. In front of the stand-alone two-car garage there was a midnight blue sports car with a Massachusetts license plate. *That must be Tony's car*, she thought. As she got out of her own car, Annie took in Wedgwood's perfectly kept lawn and formal garden, which was interspersed with straight, stone-covered footpaths and surrounded with a wrought-iron fence. There were no humble wildflowers here; cultivated roses of ivory and pink contrasted beautifully with the Wedgwood blue siding of the house. Dahlias, gladiolus, chrysanthemums, and asters bloomed amid well-groomed shrubbery. Annie sighed. She felt she'd never be able to achieve anything so refined at Grey Gables.

In the open area of the ample back lawn, a large, green-and white–striped marquee had been set up for the party that afternoon, underneath which were several long tables along with folding chairs that were placed around each one. The forecast was for sunny and hot; Annie thought an outdoor get-together was a fun idea, and the shade of the open-sided tent would be welcome by two o'clock in the afternoon. She was stopped at that thought when Gwen came outside through the side garden to meet her.

"Thank you for coming so quickly, Annie," Gwen said in a low, conspiratorial tone of voice. "I've had a bit of a ... surprise, and I want to get this all straightened out before our guests arrive this afternoon."

"What is it, Gwen?" asked Annie, almost whispering. "I'll do whatever I can to help."

Gwen's face colored a bit before she answered, "Well, Tony is here, and he's brought someone with him. ... A girl."

When Annie's face showed that she didn't understand the problem, Gwen continued, her words pouring out, "He says this girl is his fiancée! He met her in Ireland, during his tour, and now he's brought her home. And he expects her to stay here, of all things. I just can't ... I don't know ... and what will John say when he gets home from the bank at noon? I called all of the local hotels, and they're all booked. He hardly knows this girl. I just don't know what he was thinking. ... You see, our daughter Meredith and her family are here from North Carolina to stay this entire week; she and Frank, her husband, and the grandkids went to explore the downtown shops this morning before Tony arrived. Our son George and his wife, Sandra, are driving in from Portland today—they're just staying over the weekend. They should be here any time now. We wanted to have the whole family together. There just isn't room in the house for an extra person, and besides, how would it look to have her staying here with us?"

Annie began to get the picture. "Would you like her to come and stay with me at Grey Gables?" she asked.

"Oh, yes! That was just what I was hoping. Thank you so much, Annie!" Gwen gave Annie a quick hug, obviously grateful that she didn't have to ask outright for her son's fiancée to stay with Annie.

"Would you like her to come with me now?" asked Annie.

"Yes ... I think that would be best. That way she could get settled in, and she could return with you this afternoon for the party. I hope this isn't too much of an imposition, Annie. I *really* appreciate it. I was just so surprised when he showed up with her this morning and introduced her as his fiancée."

"Well, as I recall, you did say that he told you he was bringing you a surprise," said Annie.

Gwen led Annie back the way she had come, through the enclosed back porch, which was neater and more finely decorated than most people's front entry, and into the kitchen where a handsome young man and a strikingly beautiful girl sat on stools beside a granite-topped kitchen island. Both stood as Annie and Gwen entered the kitchen.

Tony Palmer was a perfect blend of his parents. He

was tall and muscular, and while he mostly favored his father in the firm set of his jaw and his brown hair, he had his mother's expressive, pale blue eyes. When he looked at the young woman standing next to him, Annie thought she could clearly read his feelings; he was not just smitten with this girl. He was in love.

Tony's fiancée was stunning, but she didn't seem to be aware of it. Her thick, reddish–dark brown hair cascaded over her shoulders, complementing her clear, peaches-and-cream complexion. She was small and delicate-looking. Her green-gold–color eyes shined with intelligence, and Annie thought, in the right circumstances, good humor. At that moment, however, her expression was guarded. Annie didn't blame her; the feeling of the awkwardness of the situation was almost palpable.

"Annie, this is my son Tony," said Gwen, "Tony, this is Mrs. Dawson."

Tony reached out to shake hands with Annie, smiling slightly as he grasped her hand. In a quiet baritone-range voice he said, "It's nice to meet you. I've heard a lot about you. Mrs. Holden was my favorite neighbor when I was a kid. I used to mow the lawn for her sometimes. She made the best oatmeal-chocolate chip cookies. I was sorry to hear that she had passed away."

"And this," Gwen paused dramatically as she waved her hand toward the girl, "is Tony's fiancée ... Drev ... I'm sorry, dear, how is it you pronounce your first name again?" Tony face registered embarrassment at his mother's gaffe.

Tony's fiancée held out her hand to Annie and said in a lilting voice with a soft Irish accent, "Hello, Mrs. Dawson.

I'm Dervla ... Dervla O'Keefe."

Annie smiled and took Dervla's hand and responded, "It's very nice to meet both you and Tony, and please call me Annie."

"Annie has offered to have Dervla stay at Grey Gables; it's just around the hill from us," Gwen said, directing the last part to Dervla.

"Mom, it's the twenty-first century, and we're engaged ... she can just stay in my room—"

"She most certainly will not be staying with you in your room, young man. Not under my roof. I don't care what century it is," Gwen said with force, the tone of her voice rising with each syllable.

"I didn't mean 'with me'," Tony said with exasperation in his voice. "I meant that I can sleep on the sofa, or on the floor in the family room for that matter. I don't understand why you're getting so upset."

Dervla reached out to touch Tony's hand and said, "Tony, it's fine. I understand your mother's reservations completely. I can find a hotel to stay at while I'm here. I'm sorry, Mrs. Palmer. We should have called to prepare you, but Tony wanted to surprise you, and we thought it would be fun. We should have realized that you might need to make other arrangements."

"Dervla, there's no need to stay at a hotel," Annie said, not wanting to reveal that Gwen had already called every hotel in the vicinity. "I have lots of room, and I'm just down the street. I'd be really happy to have you come and stay as long as you'd like."

Dervla hesitated, and looking at Tony said, "That would

be OK, wouldn't it, Tony?"

"Thank you, Annie," Gwen said with obvious relief, not waiting for Tony's reply, "and thank you, Dervla, for understanding my position."

Tony said, "If that's the way it's going to be, I'll drive Dervla down to Grey Gables and help get her settled, if that's all right with you, Annie. Our luggage is still in the car."

"But Tony, everyone will be coming home shortly—your father, and Meredith and Frank, and you haven't seen your nieces and nephew in ages. And George and Sandra should be here by lunchtime too," said Gwen.

"We'll be right back, Mother, I'm just going to help carry in Dervla's luggage."

"I thought maybe Dervla would like to stay at Annie's for a while and rest up before the party this afternoon. I thought we could just have the family together for lunch," said Gwen.

Tony's expression was grim. "She *is* family, Mother. We are going to be married. You should apologize to Dervla."

"No, Tony. It's all right," said Dervla, trying to hide her distress. "I ... I am rather tired. I can meet the rest of your family later this afternoon."

Annie looked at the trio: Tony looked like thunder, Gwen appeared unrepentant for her careless remark, and Dervla was near to tears. It seemed best to get things moving.

"It would be great if you could come and help with Dervla's luggage, Tony. The guest room is on the second floor," said Annie.

Without another word to or look at his mother, Tony

took Dervla's hand in his and said to Annie, "We'll wait for you outdoors, Annie." Then the two exited the kitchen through the back porch.

Annie looked at Gwen, wishing she could advise her. She knew that Gwen could be ... for want of a better word ... snobbish, but she'd never seen her be outright unkind. How could Gwen not see that she was hurting her son's and future daughter-in-law's feelings with her attitude? It was understandable that she was concerned about accommodations for everyone. What Annie didn't understand was how Gwen was handling the news that her youngest son was engaged. What should have been a joyous occasion was now spoiled.

But then, Annie thought, *it isn't as easy as that.* She tried to imagine how she would have received a new son-in-law if LeeAnn had brought home someone she had just met over a vacation in a foreign land. Yes ... that would have been difficult. As it was, Herb Sorenson was someone the family had known as a teenager, and it was only after the two young people had gone away to college that they fell in love and became engaged. Their announcement had been a long-expected development, and it was a happy one for Wayne and herself.

A line from an old song that was popular when Annie was young came to mind: "Before you abuse, criticize, and accuse, walk a mile in my shoes." Gwen was probably doing the best she could under the circumstances. Annie decided it was best not to speak of it for the time being. If and when Gwen wanted to talk to her about it, she'd be there for her.

"We'll be back this afternoon, Gwen," said Annie as she

headed for the back door. "I'm sure everything is going to work out for the best."

"I hope so, Annie," said Gwen.

By the time Annie came out of the house, Dervla was already seated in the passenger seat of Tony's car with the windows rolled down, as the heat of the day had started to build. Tony was leaning over, talking to her through the window. When he saw Annie, he walked over to admire the Malibu.

"This is a great old car, Mrs. Dawson. You've kept it in prime condition."

"Please do call me Annie, Tony. The Malibu was a gift from my late husband for my birthday one year. I'd hate to have to part with it, so it behooves me to take good care of it. I want it to keep it as long as I can."

As Tony opened the driver's-side door for Annie, he said, "Thanks for putting up Dervla, Annie. I really didn't think that Mom would react this way. I thought she'd be happy for me ... for us. I know that it's sudden, but I couldn't leave her behind in Ireland; I love Dervla."

"I can see that you do, Tony," Annie said, "but try to look at the situation from your mother's point of view. Dervla's a beautiful girl, but you've known her such a short time."

"I know it sounds corny, but I would have asked her to marry me the very first day I met her if I thought she would have accepted me. It's not because she's beautiful to look at; lots of women are pretty. There's something special about her that's more than skin-deep. I just knew it right away, that she was the one for me," Tony said, pausing for a moment to glance at the young woman whom he'd asked to be his bride.

He continued, "We met the first week of what was supposed to be my tour of the British Isles. I'd made my way to County Kerry after flying in to Dublin from the States, and I'd planned to see the sights in Killarney. Then, I was going to travel around the coast, before heading over to Scotland. After I met Dervla, I never moved on. I canceled the rest of my trip and stayed in town to be near her. We'd meet every day and have lunch or dinner together— sometimes both if she was free. We really have come to know each other very well—better than some people who've dated over a longer period of time, but haven't really spent as much time together as we have. We didn't waste time with small talk, but really spoke to each other about things in life that are important to us. We share a common outlook, and I'd rather be with her than with anyone else. She's wonderful, Annie. She's smart and honest and good. I love her with all my heart."

Annie looked at Tony and knew that he was sincere. Dervla was beautiful, so it was easy to imagine that he was only taken with her looks, but Annie believed that his feelings were deeper than that. Tony wasn't a child, but of course, he would want to have his family's blessing when he got married. It looked like it was going to take quite a bit to convince his mother, at least, that he was doing the right thing.

~5~

After returning to Grey Gables, Annie led the way inside, carrying Dervla's small suitcase. Dervla followed, her backpack slung over her shoulder, and next came Tony, carrying her very substantial suitcase. Annie imagined it couldn't have been very easy for Dervla to pack up to come so far for a permanent move. When Annie came to Grey Gables, it wasn't with the intention of staying on, so she had only packed as if she was going away for a short vacation. LeeAnn had had to go to Annie's house in Brookfield to send more things when it appeared that Annie would be staying longer than anticipated. She began to wonder about Dervla's family. What had her parents said about their daughter coming to the States? Would the wedding be held here, or in Ireland?

Tony interrupted her thoughts, "If it's all right, I'll just carry this up to the second floor, and then I'll head straight back to Wedgwood. I want to be there when Dad gets home."

After he had deposited the case in the second-floor hallway, Tony bounded back down the stairs with an energy that Annie envied. Taking the small suitcase and the backpack from Annie and Dervla, Tony said, "I'll just carry these up too." When he returned the second time, Annie noted that even after two trips up and down the staircase, Tony wasn't breathing any heavier than if he had just taken a stroll through the garden. Oh to be so young and fit!

Tony took Dervla's hands in his and said, "Are you sure you don't want to come home with me for lunch? It really will be all right."

"I'll be fine here, Tony. I think your mother needs a little space to get used to the idea that her youngest son is going to get married. And I am still a little jet-lagged. It will be better if I can get some rest before meeting the remainder of your family."

"They are your family now too. I know that they will love you. Please don't be discouraged by my mother's reaction. I'll be back here about a quarter to two to pick you both up."

"I'm just going to walk over to Wedgwood, Tony, so don't worry about me," said Annie.

"I think I'll walk with Annie, if that's OK. After all the traveling we've done in the airplane and the car, it will be good to stretch my legs with a nice walk," said Dervla.

"If that's what you want. I'll be looking for you." With that, Tony kissed Dervla gently on the lips and then headed out the door. "Thanks again, Annie. See you both soon."

After the front door closed behind Tony, Annie said to Dervla, "Why don't we get you settled in your room first, and then I'll see what I can rustle up for lunch."

Dervla started to reply, "That would be …" when suddenly she jumped slightly and said, "Oh!"

Looking down at the floor, Annie saw the culprit. Boots was winding around Dervla's ankles in an effort to be noticed. Both ladies started laughing, and Dervla reached down to scratch between the cat's gray ears.

"Looks like you have another new friend. This is Boots," Annie explained. "She was my grandmother's cat and has been a good companion since I came here from Texas. I mostly see her when she's hungry, which is quite often, and she likes to snuggle in my lap—usually when I'm trying to crochet."

"I love cats, but I haven't kept one for a long time. I lived in a dormitory for several years while I was at college—I graduated in June last year and returned to Killarney afterwards—but when I lived at home with my parents, we had two cats, an orange tabby named Shawn, and a black-and-white one named Queen Mab. I'd almost forgotten ..."

As her words trailed off, Dervla's expression became very sad. Annie thought that perhaps she was feeling homesick and said, "Here we are standing, when you need to get some rest, and I definitely need to get tidied up. Let me show you up to your room so you can settle in before lunch. The kitchen is down this hallway to the right, and the library is across the hall to the left; so, if you need something to eat or drink, or some reading material, you are welcome to help yourself. Please feel free to explore Grey Gables at your leisure, and make yourself at home. I'm so glad to have you here—it will be nice to have some company—besides Boots, that is."

Annie and Dervla climbed the stairs and collected Dervla's luggage from the hallway where Tony had left them, rolling the large one across the floor. Annie indicated the door of the visitor's room and Dervla entered first. When she saw the wedding dress on the mannequin, still standing uncovered next to the bed, and the veil and gloves draped across the bed, Dervla exclaimed, "Ó, *tá sé go hálainn* ... how beautiful!"

The room was just as Annie had left it on Tuesday when she hurried to get to the Hook and Needle Club meeting on time. What with getting to have lunch with Ian and Andrew Gareth that day, and all the other activities that had filled her week, she hadn't had a chance to think about her newest mystery.

"I'm sorry, Dervla. I'd completely forgotten that I left these things out. I can just move them to another bedroom."

"Oh, please don't. If you don't mind, we can just move the dress to the corner." Dervla reached out to examine one of the gloves. "What lovely handwork. Are these antiques? We Irish are known for our fine crochet. I'd almost say that these must have been worked by an Irish hand, but I might be a bit prejudiced in that regard."

Annie explained how she had found the dress and the other items in the attic, and had brought them down to the bedroom. "My impression was the same as yours," Annie said. "I do think they are very old, and there's a level of art-istry here that would be hard to match. I don't really have any idea who made them. It's a bit of a mystery."

Dervla turned her attention to the hatbox. "This is lovely too. I've seen round boxes like this, but the ones I saw were just covered with decorated paper—this looks to be hand-painted. It's a beautiful arrangement, and I like the way it's held together with ribbon and lace; the ivy twining around the edge looks almost real. Do you know what kind of flowers these are?"

Annie answered, "I know the names of most of the

flowers, but there is one I don't recognize." Pointing to individual flowers on the hatbox, Annie said, "These blue ones are Jacob's ladder; I think the little yellow flowers are primrose. Of course, those are violets. I like the greenery ... the wispy little ferns and—I didn't see this before—there's even a four-leaf clover tucked in the side of the ribbon ... just there. The lavender-color flowers that look like they have beards are pansies. These—with the pink clumps of petals and those long spindly things sticking out below—I don't know what those are. Gram has a flower guide in the library. We'll have to have a look and see if we can figure out what that last one is."

Dervla leaned forward to look at the details of the box more closely. "Don't you think the lace looks crocheted? Do you think the same person who worked the crochet, painted the hatbox?" Dervla asked.

"I don't know," Annie answered. "I admired the painting, but I really didn't examine the details that well. It could be that both were made by the same person."

"Look at this," said Dervla, pointing to a shaded area on one of the ribbon ends in the painting. "Are those letters? It looks like ... 'P.R.G.'"

Now it was Annie's turn to have a closer look. "You're right! The color of the letters blends in so well with the color of the ribbon, you'd almost have to know they were there to see them. Well, 'P.R.G.' must be the painter's initials; I can't think what else they could mean."

"Do you know of anyone with those initials?"

"No, I don't," said Annie, "but this house was built by someone whose last name started with a 'G'—Grey, Captain

Grey in fact, but his first name was Zacharias. Perhaps this was painted by a relative—a niece or a sister or something."

"Wasn't he married?" asked Dervla.

"I don't think so. To tell the truth, I really don't know; I've just assumed he was a bachelor because a friend of mine, Stella Brickson, said that he lived here alone. I only heard of him for the first time this week, so I don't know much about him. ... But I do know someone who has done research on the Captain." Then Annie explained to Dervla about Andrew Gareth and his project, and told her that he was coming over to the house on Monday to work on his painting of Grey Gables.

Dervla helped Annie move the mannequin to the corner, carefully lifting the bottom edge of the dress to prevent damage. Annie loosely folded the veil and placed it, along with the gloves, back in the hatbox.

"If it's all right with you, Dervla, I'll put the box on top of the dresser. I'll just get rid of that *awful* old hat," said Annie.

Dervla picked up the hat and laughed. "You're right about it, Annie. It *is* sort of hideous. But if you don't mind, instead of getting rid of it, will you allow me to work on it a bit, to see if I can do something with it? It might be fun, and it's worth a try."

"As you wish," Annie answered, "I'm all for recycling and reusing. Though, if you can make something presentable out of that, I'd say you're a miracle worker!"

Annie told Dervla she was welcome to put away her clothing in the dresser or hang them in the closet as needed, so she wouldn't have to live out of her suitcase, and left her to settle in.

Annie went to take a quick shower. When she was finished, she put on a light cotton floral sleeveless shift and sandals. She kept her makeup light, and her hair loose.

The morning had gotten progressively hotter as it went on, but Grey Gables seemed to handle the heat very well. The early ocean breezes that came in through the open windows had cooled the place nicely, and now Annie set about closing the windows before the outside air became too hot.

In the kitchen, she decided something light was called for since there would no doubt be food to nosh on at Wedgwood later that afternoon. After she slipped a colorful apron over her dress, she put together a large salad of romaine lettuce, spinach leaves, celery, cucumbers, and spring onions, and topped it with sliced almonds and mandarin oranges. Then she whisked together oil, rice wine vinegar, a touch of Dijon mustard, sea salt, and freshly ground pepper to make a light dressing.

Just as she finished, she heard the sound of the front doorbell. She opened it to find Alice, holding a basket with a cloth napkin draped over the top. Alice was dressed in beige capri pants and a matching top. Her long, thick auburn hair looked extra curly, and her cheeks were rosy, as if she'd been in a hothouse. "You're just in time for lunch," said Annie.

"As was my cunning plan," replied Alice as she entered. Alice took a long look at Annie's attire. "Don't you just look the picture of domesticity. For a moment I thought I must have stumbled back to the 1950s. All you need is a string of pearls around your neck."

"I just had my shower and got dressed for Gwen's get-together, and I didn't want to spoil my look with a giant splash of oil and vinegar in the middle of my dress, so I put on one of Gram's old aprons. I think it suits me well, thank you very much. What's in the basket?"

"Only the best homemade rolls you've ever tasted," said Alice. "I got the recipe from one of my clients. She served them at her Divine Décor party last week, and I convinced her to part with the recipe. The secret is to make the dough the day before and let it rise overnight in the fridge. I took it out first thing this morning, to let it warm to room temperature, and then I shaped it into rolls and let them rise. These're fresh out of the oven! It made the carriage house a bit warm, but it was worth it. Besides, I knew I could come over here to cool down while my little window air conditioner tries to overcome the heat. These really are excellent—they're so light and buttery, you really don't even need to add butter or jam." Alice lifted the corner of the napkin and the fresh-bread smell of the rolls made Annie's mouth water.

"I think those will go perfectly with the salad I just made," said Annie.

At that moment, Annie and Alice heard the creak of an upstairs floorboard, and Dervla appeared at the top of the stairs. "Dervla, please come down and meet my neighbor, and my best friend, Alice MacFarlane. Alice, this is Dervla O'Keefe, Tony Palmers' fiancée. She's going to be staying here at Grey Gables for a while." Annie didn't want to give away any more than just basic information. Even though Alice was her best friend, she didn't want to carry tales about what had occurred at Wedgwood earlier, and why Dervla was staying at Grey Gables instead of with her family-to-be.

More importantly, she didn't want to embarrass Dervla.

Alice's face registered her surprise, but she recovered quickly and smiled broadly as she reached out to shake hands with Dervla. "I didn't know that Tony was engaged. Congratulations! Have you started planning the wedding?"

"Thank you, and no, we really haven't had a chance to think about the wedding yet," said Dervla, in her lilting Irish dialect.

"You're Irish!" said Alice.

"Good catch," said Annie drily.

"Tony and I just met a few weeks ago, when he came to Ireland. I guess it's what you might call a whirlwind romance. But I love him so much, and when he asked me to come to America to be his wife, the only right answer seemed to be 'yes,' so here I am," said Dervla.

"'Dervla' … that's an unusual name. Does it have a special meaning?" asked Alice.

"Yes, it does actually. It means 'daughter of a poet.'"

"Your father is a poet?"

"Actually, it was my mother who was the poet. She published several books of poetry and was well-known in Ireland. My father, Brian O'Keefe, was a master weaver."

"Was?" asked Annie.

"Yes, my parents were killed in a car accident when I was a teenager. I'm their only child; after they died, I lived with my grandmother until I went away to college."

"I'm so sorry, Dervla," said Annie.

"It was a long time ago now, but I miss them still. I know it will always be that way. I wish they could have met Tony. They would have loved him like a son."

"How does your grandmother feel about you coming to the States and getting married?" asked Alice.

"She died last winter. I don't have any other close relatives remaining there, just a few distant cousins who live in different counties, and I don't really know them. I still have Grandmother's house in Killarney, but I'm not sure what to do with that yet. I had only just begun to try to go through her things when I met Tony. After that, everything else sort of just came to a halt, except for work of course."

"What do you do?" asked Annie.

"I work, or rather, I did work in the research library at Muckross," said Dervla. She could see that Annie and Alice didn't recognize the name so she explained. "Muckross is a tourist center located on Lough Leane—that's a lake—and it includes a historical manor house, gardens, and a traditional farm. There are workshops that specialize in crafts— weaving and pottery, and a shop that sells all kinds of Irish-made products, including hand-knit clothing. The estate is part of a larger national park. My father worked there, in the weaving workshop."

"It sounds like an interesting place," said Annie. "Is that where you met Tony?"

"No," answered Dervla, smiling, "I actually met him at a pub in Killarney where I perform on Friday and Saturday nights."

"What ... sort of performance?" asked Alice, eyebrows only slightly raised.

"I sing. There's a group of boys I knew in secondary school who have a band. It's not rock music or anything like that—we perform mostly traditional Irish songs. One fellow plays the bodhran—the Irish drum; we have a flute player who's also quite good on the tin penny whistle, and there's a fiddle player too. Another fellow plays the guitar, but it's acoustic, not electric. It's fun, and a bit of extra cash for each of us since we all have day jobs. The tourists who find their way into Mavourneen's like it, and so do the locals."

"Did you say the name of the pub is 'Mavourneen's'?" asked Alice. Dervla nodded and Alice repeated the word, trying to imitate an Irish accent. "Mavourneen's—I love the sound of Irish words. Is that someone's name?"

"Actually, the pub's name comes from a song— *Mavourneen's the Flower of Killarney*. The word itself means 'my beloved,' so it's literally *My Beloved's the Flower of Killarney*," said Dervla.

"That's a great name for the place where you met the man you're going to marry—that'll be something you can tell your children and grandchildren someday," said Alice. "I'd love to hear you sing. I always associate old Irish songs with haunting melodies and sad stories."

Dervla laughed and said, "The ballads do tend to the tragic side ... but there are many happy tunes as well. Perhaps there will be an opportunity for a song—a happy one, I hope."

Annie smiled and said, "I look forward to hearing that. For the moment, though, I think we should have lunch before Alice's excellent rolls get cold. I was thinking it might be nice to eat on the porch, so if you'd both like to help me carry a few things out, we can get set up and enjoy this fine summer day."

—6—

The three enjoyed their lunch and cleared away the dishes. Dervla insisted on washing up, so that gave Annie and Alice a chance to run upstairs so that Alice could see the wedding dress, veil and gloves, and the hatbox. She was as impressed by the workmanship as Annie had been, and though she did remember a plain mannequin in the attic when they were teens, she was sure she'd never set eyes on the hatbox before.

"You've got your work cut out for you, solving this mystery," said Alice, laughing. "You're going to need all the help you can get—don't forget about your friends. You know how much we love getting involved in your little adventures!"

"How could I forget?" teased Annie. "You'd never let me."

Alice smiled and said, "Absolutely. I consider it my mission in life. By the way … I heard that you were seen having lunch with Ian Butler and some out-of-towner last Tuesday. Do you deny it?"

"Of course I don't!" said Annie. "You've been talking to Kellie Cross from the restaurant at Maplehurst Inn, I'll wager. Or was it Peggy who told the tale?"

"Right the first time. I talked to Kellie at Magruder's when I was doing my grocery run this week. I think she's got her eye on Ian—I'd watch that if I were you; you might have some competition," warned Alice.

"I'm not 'competing' for Ian. If he wants to go out with her, or anybody else, that's none of my business," said Annie.

Alice gave Annie a mock-stern look. "Annie, don't kid yourself. Don't wait till he's dating someone else to figure out how much you care about him."

Annie opened her mouth to deny it, but something made her stop.

"A-ha!" said Alice, observing the conflict on her friend's face. "I'm just giving you a word of warning, that's all, as a good friend should. So, who was the other guy?"

Annie almost said, "What other guy?" but then she realized that Alice meant "the other guy" at the restaurant. She told Alice all about Andrew Gareth, and his plan to paint a portrait of Grey Gables.

"Keep that under your hat," said Annie, "if you would, please. He doesn't want everyone to know what he's doing, although I wouldn't be surprised to learn that the whole town knows already."

Alice laughed at that, and then said, "I'll consider it privileged information until I hear otherwise. We'd better get back downstairs and give Dervla a hand before she thinks we've deserted her."

Annie and Alice returned to the kitchen to help Dervla put away the dishes. Then they lazed around on the porch, talking and laughing and eventually falling into companionable silence as they watched the wind in the leaves of the trees and enjoyed the view of the ocean with its gently curling waves and bobbing sailboats. It was restful, and Annie was glad to see Dervla relaxing. It wasn't clear what the afternoon would bring, but Annie was sure the party was going to be a stressful event for the young woman.

Annie thought of her own daughter, LeeAnn, and it made her feel all the more motherly toward Dervla, who was making her way in the world without the support that a family provides. She obviously had friends back in Ireland, but it appeared that there was no one she could really go to for sage advice, as one would go to an older relative. Annie wondered what she would have said to Dervla—stay home where you have friends, a house, and a job, or follow your heart?

It was Alice who broke the silence after she looked at her watch. "As much as I hate to move from this spot, it's nearly two o'clock. We should think about making our way to the Palmers'."

Annie saw a momentary flicker of uncertainty cross Dervla's face, as if she was contemplating staying right where she was. But then her resolve seemed to return, and she was the first to stand. "Yes, I just want to go and freshen up a bit." With that she went inside, and Annie could hear the tap of her shoes as she tripped lightly up the stairs.

Alice leaned over close to Annie and said in a low tone of voice, "There's a lot more to this than meets the eye, isn't there? Did Gwen blow a gasket when her baby boy broke the news that he was engaged to someone he met on vacation?"

"I really can't say anything, Alice," Annie replied. "Gwen needed a place for Dervla to stay, and I was happy to be able to offer her a room. I can say, though, that I like her. What do you think?"

"I think she's lovely, but then she's not engaged to my

son, if I had one, after only knowing him for a few weeks," said Alice. "If I were his mother, I don't know that it would matter to me if she appeared to be the most fabulous girl in the world. Marriage isn't something to be entered into lightly."

"And love isn't one size fits all," said Annie. "I'm not sure that knowing someone for a long time is any guarantee of longevity when it comes to marriage. From what I've seen, Tony and Dervla have a real connection that they should be able to build on. I don't know what their plans are, but at this point they are just engaged. Perhaps the engagement will be extended, and in time, they can put Gwen's doubts to rest."

"So there was some friction there," observed Alice.

Annie smiled. "Nothing gets past you. Let's just say that Gwen was surprised and leave it at that."

With that comment, Annie and Alice heard the sound of Dervla coming back down the stairs. "I guess we have to get moving too," said Alice. "Off we go into the lions' den!"

"Shh!" said Annie, almost whispering. "I think Dervla's nervous enough as it is. Describing meeting her future in-laws as entering the 'lions' den' is not helpful!"

"Maybe Tony's got it all sorted out now," Alice said hopefully. "She is a sweet girl. I'd hate to see her get hurt."

*   *   *   *

A short time later, Annie, Alice, and Dervla were in sight of Wedgwood. Ocean Drive was already lined with parked cars on both sides for quite a distance in both directions. It looked to Annie as if the Palmers had invited half the town of Stony Point. *So much for a "few friends and family,"* thought Annie. She was able to pick out Mary Beth's SUV, and Peggy and Wally's car. She noted with satisfaction that Ian's car was parked along the street as well.

The only other members of the Hook and Needle Club unaccounted for were Kate and Stella. Annie didn't see Stella's car among the others along the street. It was a big Lincoln Continental—one couldn't miss that. She wondered if Stella would even come to an outdoor barbecue. Annie imagined that if she did, Stella's driver, Jason, would drop her at the party and come back later, rather than park along the street.

As they approached the Palmers' driveway, Annie saw that, besides Tony's car, there sat an unfamiliar luxury four-door sedan that Annie thought might belong to Gwen's other son, George, and his wife. Annie had been told that George was a lawyer in Portland. Behind George's sedan was a large SUV with North Carolina plates that Annie concluded must belong to Gwen's daughter, Meredith, and her family.

Out on the street, parked in front of the house, was a white van with the words "Grand Avenue Catering" emblazoned on the side. The three ladies could hear strains of jazzy instrumental music playing over loudspeakers, and the smell of barbecue was in the air.

Down the street, approaching from the opposite direction, Annie and Alice recognized Kate and her teen-age daughter, Vanessa, so they waited for them to catch up. Kate was dressed in similar fashion to Annie, in a pale blue linen A-line dress and sandals. Vanessa looked cute in modest shorts and a lightweight crocheted top that her mother had designed just for her.

"Looks like the Palmers have pulled out all the stops to welcome Tony home and celebrate the completion of his degree. We had to park way over on the other side of Elm Street," said Kate as she and Vanessa drew closer.

"You should have come to Grey Gables and parked there. It's probably a little closer," said Annie. "You know you'd be welcome to."

"Thanks, Annie. I didn't think of it. Next time Gwen has a party, I'll take you up on that offer," said Kate. Looking at Dervla, she said, "I don't think we've met. I'm Kate Stevens, and this is my daughter, Vanessa. Are you a friend of Tony's?"

Dervla hesitated, and Annie said, "This is Dervla O'Keefe. She's Tony's fiancée, just come over from Ireland. She's staying with me at Grey Gables."

Kate's mouth opened, but no words came out. Vanessa, however, forged ahead with aplomb, "Ireland! Awesome! I've always wanted to go there. After we graduate, my best friend and I want to take a trip to Dublin. We've been looking at different websites about places to see, and we're trying to save some money for airfare and stuff." Without missing a beat, she continued, "That barbecue smells delicious. We had a late breakfast and skipped lunch. I'm starving. Maybe Dervla and I could go see what's available. Do you mind, Mom?" Without really waiting for an answer, she linked her arm in Dervla's as if they had always been the best of friends and asked, "What part of Ireland are you from?"

Dervla smiled and fell into step with Vanessa, giving Annie, Alice, and Kate a wave as Vanessa unerringly led the way toward the smell of the food. Annie could see that Dervla was in good hands for the moment. Vanessa was more interested in hearing about Dervla's homeland, and was oblivious to the idea that there might be any controversy connected with Tony Palmer coming home engaged.

However, Kate was not so inclined. "When did this happen?" she asked after Vanessa and Dervla were out of earshot. "Didn't Gwen just say at the last Hook and Needle Club meeting how Tony was concentrating on his career right now, and didn't have a steady girlfriend?"

"This ... is a very recent event," said Annie reluctantly. "Gwen didn't know about the engagement until the two of them showed up this morning."

"So ... is Dervla someone he knew before he went away?" asked Kate.

"No," said Annie, still trying not to elaborate too much. "He met her the first week he was in Ireland."

Kate raised her eyebrows. "That must have knocked Gwen for a loop."

"He did tell his mother he was bringing home a surprise for her," said Alice. "And though I haven't seen her since she heard the news, I think it's safe to say that she was, indeed, surprised."

Annie, Alice, and Kate made their way to the backyard and entered the crowd of people milling around under the marquee. At the far end of the open-sided tent, the caterers had set up two long tables of food and drinks. Behind the food tables and outside the tent was an extra-large grill from which emanated the aroma that had enticed Vanessa; it was carefully positioned so that the light breeze would blow the smoke and heat away from the crowd.

At the opposite end of the tent, which was nearer the house, a sound system was set up, with a CD player and a microphone. Next to that was a smaller table with a large creamy-icing–covered cake accented with crimson, Harvard's school color, sitting in the center. Stacks of small plates sat on either side, and plastic forks fanned out in front of it. On the far end of that same table sat a large basket, where people had been placing their cards to congratulate Tony for finishing his degree. Annie, Alice, and Kate each slipped their cards into the basket along with all the others.

The remaining tables were placed perpendicular to the food tables. Some people were in the food-and-drink line; others were already seated, and many were standing in groups. All were visiting with fellow residents of Stony Point and with the few people from out of town. The atmosphere was very congenial; there seemed to be no hint that there was anything amiss in the Palmer family.

Annie looked to see where Vanessa and Dervla had gotten to. Vanessa had found the food table and was filling a plate with crudités and some chicken wings, but was still managing to fire away questions at Dervla. Dervla walked beside her, but didn't take any interest in the food. She seemed to be listening to Vanessa and answering patiently, but she would occasionally scan the room—looking for Tony, no doubt. Annie looked around. She didn't see any sign of Tony either.

Up nearer the house, Annie saw Mary Beth and Gwen standing in a tightly knit group, with their backs to the tent, talking with a couple who were facing her way. Annie took them to be Gwen's son and daughter-in-law. George was recognizable as a Palmer, but his features were the opposite of his brother's. George had his mother's blond hair and round face, and his father's eyes. His wife, Sandra, reminded Annie of Gwen, down to her perfectly coiffed hair and the meticulous details of her outfit. They made no sign of going to speak to Dervla. Since Gwen wasn't facing the tent, perhaps she hadn't seen Dervla when she arrived, and of course, neither George nor Sandra would know Dervla or Annie by sight. Annie just hoped that Gwen wasn't purposely ignoring Dervla; no good would come of that.

Annie smiled as she saw Ian talking to Wally on the far side of the tent. He seemed to be describing some situation in great detail, using his hands to demonstrate something she couldn't quite make out. Wally was listening, chin in his hand, as if working on solving the problem Ian was laying out. Annie knew that Wally often worked for Ian, making home repairs and sometimes taking on the job of remodeling certain areas of Ian's house, and surmised it probably had something to do with that.

Seeing Wally, Annie knew that Peggy wouldn't be far away. Sure enough, Peggy breezed in behind her, almost breathless with news. "Did you girls hear the latest? Tony Palmer is engaged! Gwen didn't say a word, but I was talking to Meredith just now while we were watching the kids play badminton, and she told me that he brought a girl home—from Ireland no less."

Alice spoke, "You're a little behind the curve this time, Peggy. Tony's fiancée is staying at Grey Gables with Annie."

"Seriously?" said Peggy. "Meredith didn't mention that.

She just said that her mother was not a happy camper. I guess Tony and his dad are in the house right now, having a deep discussion in John's study. Meredith says they've been in there since after lunch."

"I wondered why Tony wasn't out to meet us," said Annie. She explained that she, Alice, and Dervla had walked over from Grey Gables.

"Dervla? What kind of name is that?" asked Peggy.

"It's Irish," said Alice. "She said it means 'daughter of a poet.'"

"I thought the Irish speak English like we do," said Peggy.

"They do," said Annie, "but the original tongue of Ireland is Irish Gaelic, or I guess they would just say 'Gaelic.' I think it's taught alongside English in school."

"Well, whatever her name is, it's got the Palmer family in a tizzy. Where is she, by the way?" asked Peggy.

"She's over there with Vanessa, who is giving her the third degree about Ireland," said Kate. "Honestly, this is the first time I've heard anything about her wanting to take a trip to Ireland. I wonder how long she and Mackenzie have been plotting that! It's a good thing they won't be graduating for a couple of years yet. Perhaps that plan will die a natural death."

"Wow, she's gorgeous!" Peggy exclaimed. "It's no wonder she turned Tony's head."

Annie wanted to try to turn the conversation to a different topic. She'd only known Dervla since that morning, but in a short time she'd come to feel very protective of her. She was beginning to understand how Tony had formed an attachment so quickly. There was something special about the girl. Looking around for inspiration, she was a bit surprised to see that Stella had come to the party and was sitting at one of the tables talking to Reverend Wallace and his wife. Annie knew that Stella wouldn't tolerate any nonsense, and she thought the presence of the pastor might inhibit a discussion about Dervla and Tony.

"Look," Annie said, "there's Stella. We should go say hello."

"I wonder if she knows about Tony," said Peggy.

Annie just stopped herself from rolling her eyes. Peggy was a good friend, and was a lot of fun, but her penchant for gossip could sometimes go beyond the pale.

"Maybe we should just wait to see if Tony makes an announcement before we spread the news any further," said Annie.

"But it wouldn't be fair if we all know, and Stella doesn't," said Peggy. Just noticing who Stella was seated across from, she added, "... but maybe you're right. Stella might not want to hear about it, unofficially, that is."

As the group made their way to greet Stella, Annie glanced over in the direction of the house and saw Tony and his father coming toward the tent. Neither looked especially happy. John joined Gwen's group, but Tony walked past them, wordless, having seen Dervla on the other side of the marquee.

After saying hello to John, Mary Beth excused herself and came over to join the Hook and Needle Club ladies as they all seated themselves near Stella. Gwen, John, George, and Sandra seemed to draw nearer together, their heads bent in close to one another, almost like a huddle in a football game.

Annie was surreptitiously watching Tony. When he reached Dervla, he took her hand in his, and as she looked up into his face her smile became warmer, her eyes brighter. *Yes,* thought Annie, *she does love him.* There was no mistaking the look. She wished that Tony's family had been watching, but they were still in their huddle.

Then Annie noticed a blond woman who was also observing the scene. Annie felt like she was seeing a carbon copy of Gwen, only this woman was about twenty-five years younger and a bit more contemporary in her choice of clothing than Gwen. It had to be Meredith.

Annie watched her make her way toward Tony and Dervla. With his arm loosely slung around Dervla's shoulders, Tony was speaking to Vanessa; he looked up when his sister approached. His eyes looked uncertain, until Meredith said something and reached out her hand to shake Dervla's. Now both Tony and Dervla were smiling, and it did Annie's heart good to see that someone in Tony's family was welcoming Dervla.

Shortly, a man surrounded by four young children, including Peggy's daughter, Emily, entered the tent. There was a boy who looked to be about Emily's age, and two older girls. Annie felt certain that this must be Meredith's husband, Frank, and their children. This was confirmed when he made his way to stand next to his wife and proceeded to introduce himself and the children to Dervla.

Annie wasn't aware how much the others had seen, but Alice was the first to speak up, "There's Tony with Dervla now—and Frank and Meredith too."

Peggy didn't waste a moment. "Looks like the kids finished their game. I should go see about Emily and introduce
myself to Tony's fiancée." With that, she got up from her
seat and went to pry Wally away from Ian so that he could
join her.

"What did she say?" asked Stella.

"I think she said she was going to go meet Tony's fiancée," replied Mary Beth with a quizzical look on her face.
"When did this happen? I was just talking to Gwen, and she
didn't mention anything about a fiancée."

"We'll fill you in, in just a moment," said Alice. "I think
that Tony might be getting ready to make an announcement."

It did appear that Tony and Dervla were making their
way toward the area where the sound system was located.
Once there, Tony turned on the microphone, cleared his
throat and began to speak, "I want to thank you all for coming out this afternoon. Sorry I wasn't out here to greet all
of you when you arrived, but I'm glad to see you and appreciate you taking the time out of your busy schedules to be
here today.

"I've had my nose to the grindstone now for six years—
finishing up my bachelor's and now my MBA. I want to
thank my parents for their financial assistance and moral
support all this time. It was their idea that I should take a
long vacation to celebrate the completion of that phase of
my life. I expected the trip to be an ending, a capstone to
my life as a student, but fate would have it that it turned
out to be a new beginning instead." Putting his arm around
Dervla, he said, "My first week in Ireland, I met someone
very special. We spent a lot of time together talking about

our views on life, and what we want to achieve. When it was time to come home, I couldn't imagine life without her, so I asked her to marry me. Please welcome my future wife, Dervla O'Keefe."

~ 7 ~

The rest of the afternoon went past in a blur. The crowd had erupted in spontaneous applause when Tony made his announcement. Friends and neighbors lined up to wish the young couple well. It was, of course, a complete surprise to almost everyone, and there were murmurs about the short time that the two had known each other before becoming engaged, but the general tone was that of a celebration.

Many of the guests went to Tony's parents to congratulate them on the good news that their son was engaged. Annie thought that Gwen and John's expressions looked strained, but they rose to the occasion and graciously accepted the goodwill that came their way. Although Annie never did see Gwen approach the young couple that afternoon, John, George, and Sandra were cordial when they were finally introduced to Dervla, but not especially warm. It was a strange and awkward situation amidst the otherwise merry occasion.

Meredith and Frank were the exceptions in the family. Meredith in particular seemed to be doing everything she could to make Dervla feel like one of the family, and Frank kept an eye on the children so that his wife could help Tony with introductions. When Annie met Tony's sister and her husband, she found them to be exceptionally friendly and outgoing. Frank Campbell was a Southerner like Annie, and they jokingly compared accents. George and Sandra were friendly to Annie as well, but they were by nature, she thought, more reserved.

The party had been slated for two to four o'clock, but it was nearly five before the crowd really began to disperse. Stella was the first of the Hook and Needle Club members to leave, as she had instructed her driver, Jason, to pick her up at four. In typical Stella fashion, rather than standing in the queue that had formed, she walked to the front of the line to speak to Tony and Dervla before she left.

Annie had wondered if Stella would rake Tony over the coals, but instead, when it was her turn to congratulate the couple, she surprised the other ladies by complimenting Tony on his choice of a bride. She did mention to him that now he should stop roaming around and get to work. He took her advice with a smile and said, "That's just what I intend to do, Mrs. Brickson."

Ian was one of the last to offer his congratulations. The catering team, which had also provided the marquee, the tables and chairs, and the sound system, had begun the task of clean-up, and the crowd had thinned out considerably. Annie had noticed Ian throughout the afternoon, moving from group to group, charming the older ladies, chatting about sports with the men, and listening patiently as several young mothers discussed their concerns about calming traffic around the school for the upcoming school year. She even saw him kiss a baby. And it wasn't even re-election time.

After Ian had congratulated Tony and Dervla, he walked over to say hello to Annie and Alice; the rest of the Hook and Needle Club members had already left the party. Alice returned his greeting, and then smiling slyly, said that she just realized that she was "dying of thirst," and would they please excuse her so that she could get a drink before it was cleared away. Annie and Ian exchanged glances, but said nothing about her obvious intention to leave them alone together.

"So," asked Ian, "is Andrew stopping by Grey Gables next week?"

"Yes, I think so," answered Annie. "That's how we left it after lunch at Maplehurst. We arranged for Monday, but didn't set a time. I haven't heard from him yet, so I'm not sure exactly when he's coming over."

"If you'd like me to be there too, just let me know," said Ian.

"I don't think there's any need for that, but thanks for offering," said Annie.

Ian hesitated and then said, "I understand that Dervla is staying with you at Grey Gables. It was really nice of you to open your home to her."

"It's no problem. Gwen has a houseful, and I have all that extra room. Besides, Dervla is delightful. I'm glad to have her company."

"If I'm not mistaken, there's more to it than just the issue of space. I've known Gwen and John long enough to recognize when they are not entirely pleased with a situation," said Ian.

"I think it was just that they were unprepared," said Annie diplomatically. "I'm sure that when they get to know Dervla, they'll accept her and be happy for Tony."

"Maybe," said Ian. "Sometimes we Mainers can be stubborn." Changing the subject, Ian said, "Would you like to do something this evening? We could catch a movie, or just grab a bite to eat at The Cup & Saucer."

"Thanks Ian—perhaps another time. It's been an eventful day, and I'm planning to make an early night of it."

"Of course I'm disappointed, but I understand," said Ian with good humor. "Just promise me we'll set up something soon—maybe we could go out to dinner one evening—something a little fancier than The Cup & Saucer."

"That's a promise I'll be glad to make," said Annie. "I enjoyed our lunch the other day. I didn't realize you knew so much about art and history. I saw a whole new side of you, Mr. Mayor. You just keep surprising me."

Ian smiled at her praise. "I won't forget that you've promised. I'll be giving you a call."

After Ian left, Alice returned to her side and Annie said, "'Dying of thirst' ... that was pretty transparent, don't you think." It wasn't a question.

Alice's face was all innocence. "I don't know what you mean. I was rather thirsty." And then she asked, "Didn't he ask you to go out this evening?"

"As a matter of fact, he did, but I turned him down. I'm tired. It must be this heat."

Alice rolled her eyes. "Annie, what am I going to do with you? He likes you, and if I'm not mistaken, you like him. Stop putting up roadblocks."

"I'm not 'putting up roadblocks.' It has been a long day. Besides, I did promise him that we'd go out sometime soon."

Alice sighed. "I guess that's OK then."

"I'm glad it meets with your approval," Annie said with a hint of sarcasm. "Let's go tell Dervla that we're heading home."

When they went to say goodbye to Tony and Dervla, Tony said that he would bring Dervla over to Grey Gables later. He explained that the two of them were shortly heading up to Boothbay Harbor to attend evening mass at the Catholic Church, so that they could attend the Stony Point Community Church service with the rest of the family on Sunday morning. It hadn't occurred to Annie that Dervla might be Catholic; she hoped it wouldn't be another issue of contention for Gwendolyn.

As Annie and Alice walked toward home, they observed that very few cars remained along Ocean Drive. They were glad it was such a short walk from Wedgwood to Grey Gables and the carriage house. While it was still quite hot out, they could take their time and enjoy the sights and sounds of the ocean in a way that just wasn't possible when one was traveling by car.

Annie had given an extra key to Grey Gables to Dervla, so that she could come and go as she pleased. It was a good thing. Annie really did feel exhausted after all the events of the day. After taking a brief shower to cool off, she put on a lightweight caftan and curled up on the sofa to read a new mystery she'd checked out of the library. It was an exciting story, complete with a Victorian heroine and Egyptian mummies, but it wasn't long before she began to doze.

She awoke with a start and realized that the sun had set while she had been asleep. She got up and went to the kitchen to fix herself a cup of chamomile tea and snacked on a small bowl of trail mix while she waited for the water to heat up. Boots wandered in wanting attention and a treat, which Annie gave unstintingly. Then she took her book and cup of tea up to bed and read until her eyes were too tired to continue. She turned off the light and fell asleep. She only vaguely remembered hearing Dervla climbing the stairs.

*   *   *   *

Sunday morning started out much warmer and muggier than normal, and it was predicted that by the afternoon the temperature would soar into the low 90s. Grey Gables wasn't equipped with air conditioning, but the air quality tended to be slightly better inside than out.

Tony had come by very early to pick up Dervla, so that she could have breakfast with the family before going to church. He was dressed in a light gray suit and tie; she looked charming in a knee-length, empire-waist dress with cap sleeves made with a sage green print. Annie was pleased to see them dressed up for church. The custom of wearing your "Sunday best" seemed to have gone by the wayside in recent years, though it had never gone out of fashion for her.

Because of the heat, Annie dressed as lightly as she could for church that morning. She wore a short-sleeved dress with a wide waistband, made from a cotton blend in a dark blue floral print with a white background, and wore matching dark blue shoes with low heels. She smoothed back her hair into a chignon and put on a pair of blue-and-white—porcelain drop earrings.

Shortly before the service was to begin, Annie drove her

car into the church parking lot and parked in a space under the tall, leafy trees that provided shade all around the edge of it. She always derived a sense of serenity from the sight of the white-clapboard–sided church building. It was located within walking distance from Main Street, but the property was surrounded by a curtain of tall pine trees that provided a green backdrop in every season and served to separate the Sunday morning observance of creed and ritual from the workaday area of commerce.

The front doors were open, and as she walked up the steps with others who were also just arriving, she could hear the sound of the organist playing a familiar hymn. Once inside, she saw that the entire Palmer family, including Dervla, was already seated in a couple of pews on the left near the front. Mary Beth was sitting alone on the opposite side, nearer the back, so Annie slipped into the pew next to her, and they exchanged a few words about the upcoming Hook and Needle Club meeting that week.

"I have an idea for a new project for the group," whispered Mary Beth, "but there's not enough time right now; we can talk about it when the service is over."

Just as Mary Beth said "over," the organist began playing the notes of the opening hymn, and the worship hour began. Reverend Wallace gave a thoughtful sermon, as he always did. His text that day was from Ephesians 2:19, 20: "You are no longer foreigners and aliens, but fellow citizens with God's people and also members of his household, built on the foundation of the apostles and prophets, with Christ Jesus himself as the chief cornerstone."

After the closing hymn, the pastor returned to the pulpit to give the announcements. Asking Tony and Dervla to stand, he announced their engagement and asked the congregation to join him in congratulating the family. There was a burst of applause. Though many in attendance were at the Palmers' house on Saturday, just as many were not, and when the announcements had ended, Dervla and Tony were once again engulfed by well-wishers.

After they had made their way out of the church building, Mary Beth apprised Annie of her idea.

"What would you think if we plan a shower for Dervla?" asked Mary Beth. "It might be a bit early for a bridal shower—I haven't heard anything about a date for the wedding, but I got the impression from Gwen that it wouldn't be anytime soon. I thought it might be nice if we could do a 'hope chest' shower—you know, each of us make something that could be useful for her to set up household. Alice told me that Dervla is an orphan, and I don't know what she has or whether she was able to bring much in that way over with her. What do you think?"

"I think that's a lovely idea, Mary Beth," said Annie. "You can present the idea on Tuesday and see what the others think. If they agree, then we'll work out the details."

Back home at Grey Gables, Annie changed into more comfortable clothing and decided she would use the afternoon to try to complete the items that she had been crocheting, so that she could begin working on something for Dervla. The cloche for her friend in Texas was done, and the lapghan was close to being finished—she needed to crochet several more rows, weave in the loose ends, and add some braided fringe.

She thought she might set the baby blanket aside for the time being since it wasn't for someone specific. She was always wary of doing that, fearing that she would set it aside and not get back to it. The other ladies at the club often talked about their "UFOs"—their UnFinished Objects—the projects they started and hadn't finished. Gram had always insisted that she finished what she started, and that had always made her careful about beginning a new project before finishing a current one. Still, she thought, she would make an exception this time. She promised herself that after she completed something for Dervla, she would get back to the baby blanket before going on to a new project.

Annie was surprised when Dervla returned to Grey Gables late in the afternoon. She looked hot and tired. Tony had walked her to the door, but didn't come in. Dervla was quiet, and Annie resisted the urge to ask questions. Sitting in the living room as she crocheted, Annie had put on a CD of stringed instrumental music at a low volume as she worked on the lapghan. Dervla joined her; having found Annie's grandmother's flower guide in the library, she was attempting to find the unidentified flower from the painting on the hatbox. But she was restless, and after scanning a few pages she would suddenly stand and pace around the room. She declined dinner and went to her bedroom to retire early. Annie supposed she wasn't used to that sort of heat. At least she hoped that was all that was bothering Dervla.

*　　*　　*　　*

Andrew Gareth had called Annie on Sunday afternoon and arranged to come over to Grey Gables at two o'clock on Monday, so when she awoke well before six on Monday morning, all of the chores that she hadn't completed on Saturday came back to her mind. She wanted Grey Gables to look its best. In her experience, most men didn't notice the details, like dust in a corner, but she thought an artist might be more attuned to the particulars.

There was no need to throw off the covers before she got out of bed; the night did not bring appreciably cooler temperatures, and even the covering of a sheet seemed to be too much. Boots had sprawled out on the wooden floor seeking coolness instead of snuggling up to Annie as she usually did. It felt like it was going to be another sweltering day. *All the more reason to get going early*, thought Annie.

Downstairs in the kitchen, she looked out the window to see the sun's first light just breaking over the ocean. It was a "rosy-fingered dawn." A broad stripe of orange sky seemed to lie atop the violet-color sea, and above it the sky was streaked yellow, rose, lavender, and deep blue. It was a beautiful sight—*God's painting*, she thought. She also remembered the old saying, "Red sky at morning, sailor take warning." She hadn't paid attention to the forecast. She wondered if Maine was in for thunderstorms that would break the heat.

"Good morning."

Annie jumped at the unexpected sound of Dervla's voice, nearly spilling the glass of orange juice she held in her hand. She laughed. "Good morning, Dervla. I didn't hear you come down the steps—I was so enthralled with the sunrise this morning."

Dervla came to stand next to Annie to look out the window and said, "Ach, 'tis a 'glowing dawn of brighter day' I hope."

"That sounds like a line from a poem—is it from one of your mother's?" asked Annie.

"No, it's a line from a poem by Robert Burns. That was one advantage of having a mother who was a poet. She made sure that I not only read poetry, but memorized it too."

Annie smiled and said, "That's a fine gift. The things you memorize as a child stay with you forever. My parents were missionaries and made sure I memorized scripture, and it's amazing how often those words come to me, as a help in all sorts of situations."

"I memorized scripture too. My mom was especially keen on the Psalms. You're right about it—I never thought of it as a gift before. There are times when I hear her voice in my head, speaking those lines, helping me to not only learn the words, but to understand what the Poet meant. ... I ... I wish she were here now."

Tears filled Dervla's eyes and began splashing down her cheeks. Annie reached over to the table to grab a napkin and gave it to Dervla to wipe her face, and then placed her arm around her shoulders. Annie kept silent for some time. All the highs and lows of the last few days must have been building up—a proposal of marriage, leaving her home, meeting her in-laws ... it seemed best to just let Dervla have a good cry.

After a while, Annie said, "I can't replace what you have lost, Dervla, but I am here, and I am a friend. Whatever I can do to be of help to you, I will."

Dervla wiped away the tears from her face. Her cheeks

and nose were extra rosy, and her eyes were still sad and full of unshed tears, but she smiled at Annie. "Thanks, Annie, for all that you have already done. Just to have someone here who is so willing to be a friend to a stranger helps more than you know."

"I don't think of you as a stranger, and I'm glad to be your friend. No matter how things work out with the Palmers, there's a place for you here as long as you need it," said Annie. "Now, let's get some breakfast, and you can tell me your plans for the day, and I'll tell you mine."

"You know, I am hungry now. I just couldn't eat last evening. It's amazing what a good cry can do for your appetite," said Dervla.

As they prepared their breakfast, Dervla said, "I don't really have any plans for the day. Tony's father asked him to spend the whole day with him at the bank. Mrs. Palmer and Meredith are going shopping in some other town ... I can't remember the name of it."

That pulled Annie up short, and she asked without really thinking, "Didn't they ask you to go along?"

Dervla hesitated. "Meredith did. I got the impression from Mrs. Palmer that she wanted to keep it just a mother-daughter outing, so I declined. I'm not really much of a shopper anyway."

Annie could see the hurt in Dervla's expression that she was trying to brush aside as if the snub wasn't important.

Dervla continued, "After closing time, Tony's going to come by to pick me up for dinner. I ... I think his father would like him to take a job at the bank here in Stony Point."

"How do you feel about that?" asked Annie.

"It's really up to Tony. As long as we're together, it doesn't matter if it's in Stony Point or Boston, or any other place. I'll go wherever he goes."

Annie smiled. Unbidden, the words of Ruth from the Old Testament, spoken to her mother-in-law no less, came to Annie's mind, "Whither thou goest I will go." Would Gwen and Dervla ever have a relationship as caring as Naomi and Ruth?

Then Annie explained her plans for the day—the chores that needed to be done before Andrew Gareth showed up at two that afternoon.

"You must let me help with the cleaning," said Dervla, "it's the least I can do."

"That would be very helpful—thank you!" said Annie. "If you could dust the library, the living room and the dining room, I could mop the floor in here and the mudroom, and vacuum the rugs."

"Sounds like a plan," said Dervla. "It will feel good to do something useful!"

After breakfast, Annie and Dervla changed into work clothes, and swept and scrubbed and dusted and polished, going far beyond the few tasks Annie had intended. It was nearly twelve when the two of them stopped working.

Annie surveyed the results with satisfaction; she could never have accomplished so much in such a short time without Dervla's assistance. Annie thought how pleased Gram would have been to see Grey Gables looking so spiffy. Every wooden surface glowed, and the air was full of the scent of citrus from the cleaning products they had used. Grey Gables was ready to welcome the artist who was going to capture "her" likeness on canvas for posterity—it seemed only right to think of Grey Gables as a fine lady who would be posing for her portrait. Looking down at her own perspiration-soaked clothing, Annie thought, *Now it's about time the lady of the house got ready to welcome Andrew Gareth to Grey Gables.*

— 8 —

After Annie and Dervla had taken their showers and changed clothing, they met in the kitchen to set about preparing a light lunch. Because they had been so busy doing housework, they hadn't noticed that it was getting progressively darker outside until they sat down at the kitchen table. Annie got up from the table to flip the switch by the door for the overhead light.

"I wonder where Boots is," said Annie as she sat back down. "She never misses prowling around under the table when I'm eating, in hopes that the odd piece of food will find its way to the floor."

"When I was in the library, before you came back downstairs, I saw her under the desk. I tried to coax her out, but she wouldn't budge," said Dervla.

"That's odd behavior for Miss Boots. Maybe all our rushing around as we were cleaning has her spooked," suggested Annie.

After they had finish eating, as they cleared away the dishes, Annie and Dervla heard the low rumble of thunder.

"Sounds like a storm might be on its way," said Annie. "That might be what has Boots acting so strangely. Let's go outside and have a look."

Passing through the mudroom, Annie opened the back door, and she and Dervla stepped onto the flagstone patio in the backyard, closing the door behind them to keep the heat from entering the house. The air was almost suffocating with humidity and felt eerily still. The grass and the leaves in the trees ranged in appearance from deep forest green to almost black, and the sky was a smoky gray color. In the distance, they could see roiling, dark clouds, and occasional streaks of lightning as it raced across the sky. Soon the wind began to pick up, and the sound of thunder became louder.

No sooner had Annie said, "I think we'd better get inside," than giant raindrops started to fall. She and Dervla made it back inside without getting too wet, but if they'd remained a moment longer, they would've been drenched. Almost as soon as they closed the door, there was a brilliant flash of light, followed almost immediately by a deafening crack of thunder, and then the rain began to fall in wind-driven sheets.

The overhead light in the kitchen flickered several times, and then it went out completely. In contrast to the sounds of the storm outside—the rush of the wind, the rain pelting at the windows, the periodic boom of thunder—Grey Gables itself grew quiet within. The noises that accompany the use of electricity, which normally fade into the background un-noticed, ceased, and the silence called attention to their absence. The only sound that seemed to remain inside the house was the tick-tock of the antique clock hanging on the kitchen wall.

It was dark inside Grey Gables—not as dark as night, but dark like a late, winter afternoon in Maine when the sun sets shortly after four o'clock. Annie reached into a crock she kept on a shelf over the sink and pulled out a box of wooden matches. From under the hutch, which she and Alice had previously moved from the attic, she pulled out a variety of candles—pillars, votives, a bag half full of tea lights—along with various candleholders and put them on the kitchen table. Indicating the candles, Annie said, "I'll leave these out in case the power doesn't come back on soon; we may need them tonight. I'll try to call the power company once the weather settles down a bit. I hope you don't mind storms," said Annie, lighting a pillar candle and placing it in a small clear-glass dish shaped like a sunflower.

"Not as a rule," said Dervla, "but this is a bit more extreme than I'm used to." She winced as there was another loud crash of thunder. "We get a lot rain in Killarney, but not so many thunderstorms."

"Maybe it won't last too long," said Annie. Picking up the sunflower dish and candle she had just lit, she continued, "Let's put this out in the hallway and relax a while in the living room. There's not much we can do until the storm blows over and the power is back on."

The hallway tended to be darker than the rest of the house, since the only direct natural light at the front came through the long, narrow windows on either side of the front door and the fan-shaped panes of glass in the top part of the door, and at the back through a single, tall, lace-curtained window. Indirect lighting came through the doors that led to the various rooms that bordered the hall, but that added very little to the light level during the storm. When Annie placed the candle on the hall table near the entry, the oval mirror on the wall behind the table reflected the flame and sent a bit more light into the space. The balusters along the staircase cast long, wavy shadows up the stairwell. The effect was rather eerie.

As Annie and Dervla settled into two comfy, upholstered chairs in the living room, the rain continued its downpour outside, and the wind shook Grey Gables. Dervla seemed a little nervous, so Annie thought some conversation would take her mind off the storm.

"Have you and Tony decided anything about your wedding yet?" asked Annie.

"N ... no, not really. Of course, I've thought about it, but everything has happened so fast there hasn't been time to really make any decisions," answered Dervla.

An idea popped into Annie's head. "What kind of dress are you thinking of?" she asked.

"Something traditional, I suppose, but not too flamboyant. I don't want a big hoop skirt and meters of tulle—I do know that much!"

"What do you think of the wedding dress I found in the attic?" asked Annie.

"It's lovely. I think something similar to that would be just the thing for me," answered Dervla.

"That's just what I was thinking. Let's go upstairs, and you can try it on!" said Annie. "I think it would suit you very well."

Dervla looked confused for a moment. "You mean, you would let me wear that dress for my wedding?"

"Yes, that's exactly what I mean, and the veil and gloves as well," answered Annie. "Our first order of business, though, is for you to try it on to see if it really is what you want. And if it needs to be altered, ... well, we'll cross that bridge when we come to it."

"Oh, Annie, thank you—I hope it does fit; it would be perfect," said Dervla.

"Let's go!" said Annie. With that Annie stood up and grabbed Dervla's hands to pull her out of her chair. "This is going to be fun!"

Upstairs in Dervla's bedroom, the storm continued to rage outside and the light through the window was still rather dim, but they could see well enough for their purposes. Annie and Dervla moved the mannequin from the corner so that they could remove the dress. The back opening was closed with a series of closely set covered buttons that fastened with tiny fabric loops; Annie started unfastening those while Dervla worked on unfastening the buttons on the cuffs, which matched those on the back.

Dervla finished first, so while Annie was still working on the back buttons, she changed into a slip—she only had a short one. She and Annie discussed whether it would be better to make a long petticoat to go under the dress or to try to buy one. Annie was in favor of making one, to keep in line with the handmade details of the dress. Dervla said she didn't have much experience with sewing, but if Annie would give her a hand, she'd be willing to give it a try.

Once the buttons were all undone, Annie removed the dress from the mannequin and helped Dervla slip the dress over her head and arms. Then she began the process of re-fastening the back buttons while Dervla worked on the buttons on the cuffs. When Annie had finished placing the last loop over the last button at the top of the opening, she said, "I think this would be nearly impossible to do by yourself.

These look lovely, but thank God for the man who invented zippers!"

Dervla laughed at Annie's comment, and Annie thought how good it was to hear her laugh. There had been too little of that since she'd arrived in Stony Point.

Just then, Annie heard an insistent knocking sound. "What on earth—?" she started to say, and then she realized it was coming from the direction of the front door. Annie's eyes grew wide. "Oh! I completely forgot that Andrew was coming over!" With that, she raced out the bedroom door and down the stairs to open the front door. She wasn't sure how long Andrew had been standing on the porch, but fortunately, he looked as if he had been prepared for a hurricane. He was wearing a hooded yellow rain slicker that covered him for the most part, along with waterproof boots. Over his shoulder he carried a large vinyl-sided bag.

"Oh Andrew! Please come in," said Annie. The candle flame flickered and Annie shivered. The air outside was no longer hot. The temperature must have dropped twenty degrees. She closed the door as quickly as she could once Andrew had stepped inside.

"I rang the doorbell twice, but when there was no answer, I started knocking."

"The power has gone out, so it wouldn't have been working. I'm so sorry, Andrew ... I should have called you to let you know, but with the outage and ... I just got sidetracked and forgot you were coming. Here, let me take your coat."

The floor surrounding Andrew was dotted with small puddles of water where it had dripped down from the slicker. After he had taken the coat off, Annie said, "I'll take that back to the mudroom and hang it up to dry."

Returning from the back of the house, Annie brought along a couple of towels—one for the floor and one for Andrew, though he didn't appear to need it. He had slipped out of his boots and stood waiting at the bottom of the staircase in his stocking feet.

"I'll just mop this—" began Annie.

As she spoke, a floorboard creaked loudly at the top of the stairs. Annie and Andrew both looked up at the same time. Standing near the top of the staircase was a figure in white. It was Dervla. She seemed to glow in the dim light. She had finished buttoning the cuffs of the dress, and had put on the veil and the gloves as well. The crocheted flowers and leaves wreathed her dark hair like a crown, and the delicate veil billowed around her long tresses like a net made of gossamer. The dress could have been custom-made for her; the bodice and narrow waist hugged her form, and beneath her waist the full skirt fell in gentle folds to the floor. The gloves fit her hands perfectly as she grasped the skirt and seemingly began to float down the stairs.

Annie was amazed. The wedding dress was beautiful before, when it was just hanging on the mannequin, but now, on Dervla, it was as if the whole ensemble had come to life. No longer just inanimate objects, it seemed that each part of the outfit had become an extension of her being. Annie stole a sideways glance at Andrew. Her own feelings apparently were nothing compared to his, if his countenance was anything to go by. He had grown pale, as if he had seen a ghost, and Annie feared that he might actually faint.

"Andrew, are you all right?"

He seemed to have been struck speechless, and could only stare at Dervla, entranced by the apparition before him. He only came to his senses when Dervla spoke to him with concern, not realizing it was she that was having this effect on him.

"Are you all right, sir?" she said in her lilting Irish accent as she reached the bottom step and touched his shoulder. "Perhaps you should sit down. May I get you a glass of water?"

At her touch, Andrew seemed to recover himself, though he still looked rather pale. "No. No, thank you. I'm fine. You … you just took me by surprise. If I may ask, who are you?"

"I'm Dervla O'Keefe, sir. And you are … ?"

Annie broke in, "Let me introduce you. Andrew, this is Dervla O'Keefe, fiancée of Tony Palmer, son of my friends and neighbors, Gwen and John Palmer. Dervla, this is Andrew Gareth, the artist—the extraordinary artist, I might add—who is going to be making a painting of Grey Gables."

Reluctantly, it seemed to Annie, Andrew moved his eyes from Dervla's face to acknowledge her compliment. "Thank you, Annie. I hope that I will do justice to Grey Gables." Turning back to Dervla and gently taking her hand in his, he said, "And it's lovely to meet you, Miss O'Keefe. I detect an Irish accent—what part of Ireland are you from?"

"I hail from County Kerry … Killarney specifically," said Dervla.

Andrew seemed to consider this carefully before continuing, but didn't pursue it; instead he changed the subject. "I seemed to have come in the middle of a fitting. If you'll allow me to say so, your choice for a wedding dress couldn't be more perfect."

"Thank you, sir. It was Annie's idea."

Annie took a few minutes to explain to Andrew about finding the dress and the hatbox in the attic, and that it had occurred to her as they were talking about the wedding that Dervla might like to wear the dress when she got married.

"Well done, Annie," said Andrew. "It suits her." He continued, "I probably shouldn't have come out in this weather, knowing that I couldn't do any sketching outside, but I was anxious to see Grey Gables from the inside too."

Just then there was a series of loud knocks at the door. All three were startled at the unexpected sound. Annie looked through the side window to see Tony Palmer standing at the door.

"It's Tony!" said Annie.

"Oh no!" said Dervla, "He can't see me in the dress before the wedding—it's bad luck!" And with that she turned and climbed the stairs as quickly as she was able in the long dress.

Though the rain was still coming down in buckets, the wind seemed a little less violent, and the thunder had reduced to a distant rumble. Tony continued to knock, not realizing that he had been seen. Annie didn't say anything— she hated to make him stand outside, but she waited until Dervla was out of sight before she opened the door.

Tony wasn't dressed for the weather as Andrew had been, wearing only thin dress slacks, a cotton shirt with a button-down collar, and a tie; he was absolutely soaked through.

As soon as she opened the door, Tony started talking,

"Annie! Where is Dervla? The storm … . Is she OK? I left the bank early. I tried the phone, but my call wouldn't go through."

Fortunately, Annie still held the towels in her hands that she had brought out for Andrew. After getting him to come inside, she wrapped one of the towels around Tony's shoulders and said, "She's fine, Tony. She's upstairs. The power went out. My cordless phone doesn't work without electricity. I'll give you the number for my cell phone. But first, you need to get out of that wet clothing. Go home and have a hot shower and put on some dry clothes. Then come back to see Dervla … and bring an umbrella."

"Why can't I see her now?" asked Tony.

"She's changing her clothes. I asked her to try on … something," replied Annie.

Tony just noticed Andrew. "Who are you?" he asked, somewhat rudely.

Annie introduced the two men. Tony was not making the best impression, and Andrew was less than friendly toward him. After more coaxing from Annie, Tony finally agreed to go on home to Wedgwood to shower and change.

"I'll be back in twenty minutes," he said, giving Andrew a look that seemed to say he hoped that he wouldn't see him when he returned. The two men had seemed to have taken an instant dislike to one another.

As soon as Annie closed the door behind Tony, Dervla leaned over the upstairs railing and called down, "Annie? Is he gone?" When Annie confirmed that he was, Dervla said, "Can you come up and help me get out of this? I can't get all of these buttons undone."

"I'll be right there, Dervla," she called up the stairs. Then to Andrew she said, "Would you excuse me? Please make yourself at home in the living room, and I'll be back down in just a couple of minutes."

"Take your time, Annie," he said. "I'll just use the towels to wipe up the water from the floor first."

Annie thanked him. Besides the small puddles left from Andrew's entrance, there was now a large area of water left from where Tony had been standing.

Annie had just started up the steps when she heard the familiar whir of the refrigerator as it came back to life; she leaned over the banister to see light shining from the kitchen.

"The electricity is back on!" she exclaimed. She came back down the steps and walked over to flip the switch that illuminated the hallway and the staircase, and blew out the candle. "Feel free to turn on a couple of lamps in the living room, Andrew."

Annie went upstairs to help Dervla get out of the wedding dress, and then they returned it to the mannequin and put away the gloves and veil. Leaving Dervla to finish changing clothes, Annie found Andrew studying the "Betsy Original" that hung in the hallway halfway between the living room and the library. Betsy Holden had been a first-rate designer and cross-stitcher, and this one was a prized possession of Annie's since it was her grandmother's very first design. The country scene it portrayed contained intricate details that gave it a photographic quality, and yet it was very painterly too.

"What do you think of it?" asked Annie. "Before you answer, you should know that it was designed and stitched by my grandmother."

Andrew smiled and said, "I was just about to comment on what a skilled hand the creator of this had. The nuance of the colors really brings the scene to life. It has depth and a sense of movement which is very difficult to achieve. Your grandmother was a fine artist."

"Thank you, Andrew. That means a lot coming from you." Annie paused and then continued, "So, where would you like to start your guided tour of Grey Gables?"

— 9 —

ndrew left the "itinerary" of the tour to Annie, so she decided to start at the back of the house in the library. Annie was sure that the details of the room were original to the house—the solid, dark oak bookcases were permanently built in, as was the window seat where she had spent many an hour reading when she was a child, during her visits to Grey Gables in the summers.

The room was somewhat cluttered, but that was the way that Annie had always remembered it. Both her grandparents had kept writing desks in the room. Gram used hers for writing letters and working on sketches for her designs. Gramps had been a veterinarian and kept a log of all of his cases, including various anecdotes of his experiences. One of her fondest memories was sitting in the window seat reading as Gram and Gramps sat writing at their desks. She hadn't had the heart to change the arrangement, so she left the desks where they were.

"I like this room," said Andrew. He ran his fingers over the molding along the edge of one of the bookcases and examined the intricately carved pattern along the top facing board of each section. It reminded Annie how glad she was that Dervla had been around to help with the housework— the woodwork was shiny and dust-free!

"Do you mind if I do a few sketches?" asked Andrew.

"Not at all," replied Annie.

Andrew opened the vinyl-sided bag he had carried in with him and took out a large pad of drawing paper with a rigid back and a tube-shaped leather case, from which he extracted two drawing pencils. Helping himself to the brown leather, rolling desk chair from Gramps's desk, he moved it across the room to face the window seat and sat down. With his left ankle resting on his right knee, he propped his pad of paper across his legs and began to sketch.

Trying to stay out of the way, Annie stood to one side, scanning the titles of the books on the shelves, smiling at her remembrances of so many of them that she had read. Gram had all the classics that young girls should read— *Little Women, Pride and Prejudice, Jane Eyre, Heidi, Anne of Green Gables* ..., but her grandfather made sure she was well-supplied with "boys" classics as well. She had reveled in the adventures of Jim Hawkins among the pirates in *Treasure Island* and the story of young Arthur in *The Once and Future King*. Those, along with so many other stories by authors like Rudyard Kipling, Jules Verne, and Mark Twain, had fed a love of reading that she had maintained to that day. It occurred to her that she might revisit a few of those beloved books; she was certain that she would enjoy reading them now as much as she did then, and perhaps even more.

Besides fiction, there were plenty of nonfiction books as well—her grandfather's veterinarian medicine books, a set of encyclopedias from the early 1960s, books on art and history, a couple of dictionaries, various reference books covering things like geology and astronomy, and there was a large collection on more mundane topics like sewing and gardening. Next to the flower guide that Dervla had replaced on the shelf after she'd looked at it on Sunday was an old, worn-looking book called *The Language of Flowers.*

Annie had just reached out to pull the book off the shelf when the doorbell rang. She excused herself to go and answer it, though Andrew barely seemed to notice. At the door was Tony, closing the umbrella that he had used this time coming from his car. His hair was still wet, but he was dressed in dry clothes—blue jeans and a henley-style shirt. At the sound of the doorbell, Dervla had come downstairs too. She was back in her normal attire—light slacks and a short-sleeved top. She was lovely as always, but Annie still had in her mind the vision of Dervla in the wedding dress. Annie imagined the impact that it would make when Dervla finally did walk down the aisle. She wondered when that would actually happen.

The rain had begun to taper off, and it looked like the clouds were beginning to clear away. The temperatures were cooler, and the air felt lighter. Tony and Dervla decided to go downtown and wander about the unique stores located along Main Street, saying that they would eat dinner at The Cup & Saucer that evening.

After they had left, Annie thought a cup of tea might be just the thing for a rainy afternoon. On her way to the kitchen to put on some water to heat, she asked Andrew if he would care for a cup. Barely looking up, he said, "Yes, thank you," and continued with his drawing. Annie could see that he had finished the basic outline of the room and was filling in details. It was amazing how quickly he worked.

In the kitchen, Annie first put away all of the candles

and candleholders she had set out on the kitchen table earlier when she had thought the electricity might be off for an extended period. As she set about making the tea, Annie wondered if she would be able to broach the subject of Captain Grey with Andrew to see what she could learn about him and his family, if he even had any. Perhaps Andrew had come across someone in his research with the initials from the hatbox—P.R.G. But it seemed that Andrew was intent on making sketches, so discussing the original owner of Grey Gables might be a distraction he wouldn't care to indulge in for the time being.

Annie supposed studying what Grey Gables was like on the inside was the same thing as studying human anatomy in order to be able to draw a person properly—it was important to understand the underlying structure in order to make the drawing look realistic. She didn't quite see how that would work with a house, but he was the artist; he must have had some purpose for being so interested in all the little architectural details of Grey Gables.

The whistle of the tea kettle interrupted her thoughts, and she removed it from the heat. She had already warmed the teapot with hot water from the tap, and after letting it set for a few minutes, emptied it and measured in the loose tea leaves—a teaspoon for each cup, plus "one for the pot" as she had always been told. She had purchased the specially blended tea when she and Alice had visited a new local restaurant—Lilia's Tea House—where they enjoyed an authentic "high tea," complete with cucumber sandwiches, scones, and tea cakes.

Remembering that delicious meal, Annie checked her

cupboards. All she had to offer Andrew by way of a snack were some rather stale sugar cookies she had purchased a month ago. She wished she'd thought to make something earlier ... but she'd been so busy cleaning, and then the power had gone out. *Well, that's a good excuse*, she thought.

Then she contemplated getting out some of her grandmother's best china—her Aster Blue teacups—from the cabinet in the dining room, but realized it might be more practical to just use a couple of her nice floral porcelain mugs instead. At least she didn't have to offer him tea in the set of mugs she'd found in Gram's cupboard that were emblazoned with "Portland Sea Dogs" and a ferocious-looking dog with a baseball bat in its mouth. Knowing her grandfather's love of baseball, she thought he must have picked them up at one of the many games he attended. She just couldn't see her grandmother buying a set like that. But then, she reminded herself, Gram could surprise a person.

She was just about to go ask Andrew if he wanted sugar or honey, or if he put milk in his tea, when he stepped into the kitchen. Glancing about, he said, "Looks like there's been some remodeling done in this room."

It was true. That was one of the first things Annie did after she had arrived and had determined that she would be staying for a while. It had taken weeks of painstaking work to remove the built-up layers of old wallpaper that her grandmother had added over the years. Annie had chosen to redo the walls with paint in a brightening pale yellow shade called Jersey Cream. Wally had refinished the cabinets and replaced the old tile counter with a new, high-tech one that resisted heat and scratches, and had the look of granite.

Then Annie had purchased new appliances, staying away from the current popular look of stainless steel and chrome. She had kept ceramic finishes that would fit in with the original decor. The redo was fresh and new, but still in keeping with the character of Grey Gables.

"Yes," said Annie, "it was long past due for a change. Shall we sit at the kitchen table and have our tea? Then I can show you the rest of the house afterward. After that, if you'd like to do more sketches, you're welcome to do as you please."

After they were seated, and Annie had poured out the tea, Andrew said, "Thanks, Annie, for being so accommodating. As I mentioned when we met, I have a special interest in Captain Grey and Grey Gables. It's fascinating to see the plans 'in the flesh' so to speak."

"What do you mean by 'the plans'?" asked Annie.

"While I was researching Grey Gables, I came across the name of the architect who designed it. Turns out the firm that he established near the end of the nineteenth century still exists in Boston, so I went there, and luckily, they have an archive for the original plans for every building the firm has designed—including Grey Gables. They were good enough to allow me to purchase copies of all the plans—floor plans, schematics, elevations … it's all there, including the plans for the carriage house. Speaking of which, do you know the people who live there? I'd love to get a close-up look at it as well."

"I think I can be of help to you with that," said Annie, smiling. "It just so happens that my best friend, Alice MacFarlane, lives there. I don't think there would be any problem with you having a look sometime. I think she's got a party planned this evening, so she'll be getting ready for that, but I'm sure another time can be arranged."

Andrew looked quizzical. "She's your best friend—aren't you invited to her party?" he asked.

"Oh, no," said Annie, "it's not that kind of party. It's her job—she arranges these 'parties' in other people's homes to sell products—home decor ... things—and jewelry. The person who has agreed to be the host invites her friends to her home. Alice displays the products, and the guests can purchase what they like out of a catalog."

"Doesn't sound much like a party to me," said Andrew.

"It's actually kind of fun. There's always good food, and you get to visit with friends and meet new people. And you get to see all kinds of things that inspire you to decorate or try a new style."

Andrew still looked skeptical.

"I guess it's a girl thing," said Annie.

"I'll take your word on that," said Andrew. "I've been a traveling bachelor nearly all my adult life. I have two sisters, and quite a few nieces, but I don't really see them, or any of my extended family for that matter, except at Christmastime—I usually try to make it home then. I'm the youngest of a large family, and most of my brothers and sisters still live close to where we grew up in Washington state. I don't get back there as often as I'd like to. It's not a situation that I desire; it's just a byproduct of the life I've chosen."

"So, have you never considered getting married?" asked Annie. Almost immediately, Annie realized she'd crossed over the line and before he even had a chance to answer, she said, "Andrew, I'm so sorry. I didn't mean to ask something so personal. We hardly know each other. I didn't mean to pry."

"It's OK, Annie," said Andrew, smiling. "I'm not offended. When I met you and Ian at the restaurant, I could tell right away that you are a sympathetic person. I know you're not asking just to gather gossip. The way you treat other people shows that you really care about them. I think that's probably one of the reasons that Ian is so taken with you."

Annie blushed. "We're really just friends. I don't know why people keep saying that."

Andrew looked at her sideways, "Oh, come on, Annie, I think you do know. I've seen how you look at him, and how he looks at you. I don't know much about your situation, but if there's something holding you back, try not to let it hold you back too long. Love doesn't wait forever."

"Doesn't it? You sound like you know something about that," said Annie.

Andrew looked down. "I was in love once. It was a long time ago." He picked up his mug and took a long drink of tea as if it were something stronger. "I know that she loved me too, but I had this 'brilliant idea' that I was going to travel all over the United States and do something important with my paintings."

"And you have done something important," said Annie.

"Thanks, Annie. ... Sometimes, when I remember her, I wonder if I did the right thing by breaking it off," said Andrew. "That said, I must admit that most of the time, I still feel the same rush that I felt when I first began this project. I love all the aspects of my work—the research and the painting. I guess even then I must have loved it more than I loved her. I said goodbye and never really looked back." He paused and then said, "I hope I don't come across as heartless as that sounds, but I knew that it wouldn't be fair to ask her to adapt to my way of life. She loved her home too much."

"You never saw her again?" asked Annie.

Andrew hesitated, as if remembering something that he considered telling Annie, but then changed his mind. "No. I didn't see her again. About twenty years ago, or really, more than that now, I … I learned that she married. And then, just a few years ago I read that she had died," said Andrew quietly. Though he was looking down at the table, Annie could see the sadness in his body language as he continued, "I made my choice, and I know it was the right one for both of us. There's no changing the past."

There it was again. Another person, like her, who had to come to grips with choices made, that couldn't be altered now. She thought about how soul-searching was something everyone has to do at some point, and it isn't always easy, especially when it's no longer possible to make restitution for a hurt inflicted, or apologize for a mistake made. That is, if it was a mistake that Andrew had made. Perhaps it really was the best thing for both of them. Who knows where choices will lead at the beginning of life's road? Not mere humans.

Annie patted his hand. "Maybe it would be good if we continue on our tour of Grey Gables."

Andrew looked at Annie. "You know, you really are someone special. I haven't talked with anyone about Cara in years. It's good to remember, as much as it may hurt." He stood up. "Yes, let's see the rest of your great old house."

Annie showed Andrew around the rest of the downstairs, and he took the same interest in all the architectural details that made Grey Gables as special on the inside as it was on the outside. Annie could tell he was mentally making notes on all the things he would sketch later. It seemed that he had forgotten their conversation and was now completely engrossed in what he was seeing. He really did love his chosen profession.

Upstairs, Annie opened the doors to all the bedrooms, explaining that the room with the bright pink dresser had been hers when she visited in the summers. She told Andrew how she had pleaded with Gram and had finally convinced her to let her paint it. What fun she and Alice had had picking out that particular color. It didn't suit her tastes now, but she didn't want to change it. Just seeing it made her smile.

Her mother's old bedroom still had the same wallpaper from the time of her mother's youth. It was a tiny rose pattern on a cream-color background and unfortunately showed its age. Annie knew that at some point she would need to replace the wallpaper. She hoped it came off the walls easier than the kitchen wallpaper had. She also hoped that she could find a pattern that was very similar. It always made her think of her mother, who had loved roses.

"Be sure to check out the view from the windows in the master bedroom," Annie told Andrew. "The architect placed the house to the best advantage for glorious views all around, but I think that one is the very best. It has a splendid view of the ocean."

Andrew seemed to take in every detail—the shapes of the rooms, the positions of the windows and doors, and the woodwork, which was all original to the house. He looked through every window to see the views that each room afforded. After spending several minutes looking at the ocean through the windows in the bedroom that had been Annie's grandparents' room, Andrew turned his attention to the visitor's bedroom.

Annie said, "This is Dervla's bedroom for the time being, but I don't think she'll mind if you have a look."

"If you don't mind my asking," said Andrew, "why is Dervla staying here and not with her future in-laws?"

Annie didn't want to say too much about the situation, so she tried to keep it brief. "Umm ... there were space considerations, and I have lots of room here, so I offered to let her stay at Grey Gables." It was the truth. Of course, it wasn't the whole truth, but Andrew didn't really need to know that Gwen was anxious to find pretty much any place for Dervla that didn't include her staying at Wedgwood.

"What makes me think there's more to it than you're saying?" asked Andrew.

"Isn't there always?" Annie admitted. "The engagement was ... a bit of a surprise to Tony's parents. ... They're good people. Gwen's a close friend of mine. ... But Tony just met Dervla in Ireland a few weeks ago. I don't think that the Palmers are quite prepared to accept her, as of yet. Though, to be fair, Tony's sister Meredith and her husband have been very welcoming."

Andrew actually looked grim. "I can't say I was all that

impressed with Tony Palmer. I know I only met them both once, but I hope he's good enough for her."

It seemed an odd thing for a relative stranger to say, but Annie let it pass. Andrew walked into Dervla's room and looked around, taking in the layout of the room and two of its contents in particular—the dress on the mannequin and the hatbox, which was sitting on the dresser.

When Annie first saw the dress, her inclination was to draw closer to see the details, and it was only after she had taken a closer look at the crocheted parts of the dress that she then stepped back for a more complete view. Andrew did just the opposite. He didn't go up close to the dress, but stood back a few paces, trying to get a sense of the impact of the whole thing.

While he was looking at the dress, Annie noticed a photograph Dervla had put on the nightstand next to her bed. At first she thought it was a picture of Dervla embracing another man, but when she looked closer she could see that it wasn't Dervla at all, though the woman could have passed for her double. The style of clothing that the couple wore indicated that the picture was not recent. She wondered if these were Dervla's parents.

She was drawn away from her speculation when Andrew asked, "I believe you told me earlier that you thought that the wedding dress is an antique ... do you have any idea how old it might be?"

"It may be from the turn of the previous century. It's kind of hard to say. An older friend of mine, Stella Brickson, suggested that the dress and the hatbox might be some of the things that remained in the house after my parents bought it after the death of Captain Grey."

Andrew looked over at Annie. "Why does she say that?"

"I'm not sure. Maybe because of the description I gave the ladies at the Hook and Needle Club. From that, she might have thought it sounded like it was from his era. I don't know. I thought at the time that it seemed strange for her to make a guess like that. Another thing that's strange— Alice says she remembers the mannequin from when we were teenagers, but there was no dress on it then, and neither of us remembers seeing the hatbox before. My grandmother was a great one to encourage women to put forth their needlework skills. She always felt that the womanly art of adding value and beauty to the home was underappreciated. It seems odd that she would hide something like this—that is such a fine example of talent—away in the attic. There are so many things that don't add up."

Andrew went to stand in front of the dresser, studying the painting of the flowers on the hatbox. Annie walked over to stand next to him.

"Of course, this is the hatbox I found in the attic. The gloves and veil are in it. Both Dervla and I thought the painting is lovely, don't you agree?"

"Yes, it is very nicely done," said Andrew.

"We ... actually, I should say, Dervla found some letters hidden in the painting—there on the ribbon—you can just barely make them out—P.R.G. We thought perhaps that if the dress was from Captain Grey's belongings that had been left at Grey Gables, that the box might have been painted by a relative—P.R. Grey. Have you come across anyone with those initials in your research?"

Annie was looking at the box, and when Andrew didn't answer, she looked up at him. He was staring at the box, and for the second time that day, his face had gone pale, though this time he looked less shocked and more ... she wasn't sure ... astonished?

"Andrew—what is it? Are you OK?"

Andrew seemed to regain himself. "It's ... it's nothing, Annie. I mean, I'm fine. I ...I'll have to check about those initials and get back to you." Looking around the room he said, "You know, I am feeling rather tired. Guess I've been burning the candle at both ends. I've been working in the studio late into the night. Maybe I should head back to the hotel."

"Of course," said Annie. "I'm home most days, and anytime I'm here, you're welcome to come and work on your sketches. Just give me a call. And if I'm not at home, feel free to come and sketch the exterior whenever you like."

"That's very generous of you, Annie. I'd like to sketch Grey Gables from all sides, before I decide on the angle to use for the main portrait," said Andrew.

In the upstairs hallway, seeing the door that led to the attic reminded Annie to ask, "Oh! Did you want to see the attic? I'm afraid it's a mess. It's so full of things that my grandmother saved, that it's taking me a long time to get it organized. I've begun to wonder if I'll ever finish."

Andrew laughed softly, "I would like to see it, but if you don't mind, let's wait until next time. And don't worry about the mess; that just makes it more interesting."

"That's a good way to look at it," agreed Annie, smiling. "I am no longer going to call the attic 'a mess'; from here on out, it is my 'interesting attic.' That sounds much better!"

While Andrew gathered his drawing materials from the library, Annie retrieved his yellow slicker, now completely dry, from the mudroom. The rain had stopped, so Andrew threw the slicker over his arm and slipped back into his boots, once again thanking Annie for her cooperation before heading back to Maplehurst Inn.

After he left, Annie thought about the two rather odd reactions that Andrew displayed that afternoon—first, to Dervla in the wedding dress, and then to the letters that were painted on the hatbox. She knew that he was more than just surprised when Dervla appeared at the top of the stairs; he seemed to be genuinely shocked, but she couldn't figure out why. And she was certain that the initials P.R.G. meant something to him. He had mentioned a couple of times that he had a "special interest" in Captain Grey. She wished that she had followed up and asked him why, but she wasn't so sure that he would have told her anyway.

~ 10 ~

The next day, Tuesday, Annie had a lengthy list of things to accomplish before the Hook and Needle Club meeting. At the top of the list she had written: "Take wedding dress, veil, and gloves to cleaners on Oak Lane." She had called Mary Beth the previous evening to get her advice about the best place to have the antique clothing cleaned. Annie had thought about trying to do it herself and tried to look up some information on the Internet, but there were so many different suggestions, she decided that she would rather not take a chance. Mary Beth assured her that Expert Cleaners on Oak Lane knew all about how to clean antique clothing without damaging it.

Next on the list was getting the cloche and lapghan she had finished on Sunday packaged and dropped off at the post office so it could be on its way to her friend in Texas. On down the list there were various and sundry other items that didn't look like much on paper, but always seemed to take a lot of time: fill the car with gas, stop by the bank, return library books, pick up lightbulbs at the hardware store, and then there was a short grocery list. The fortunate thing was that she didn't need to do everything before the meeting. If she got half the list completed in the morning, she would count herself well off.

Dervla and Tony had plans to go hiking with Meredith,

Frank, and the kids. They were all going to make a day of it and had taken along a picnic lunch. Fortunately, though the storm had left some wind damage in its wake, it also left behind a more pleasant, less humid air quality. It was a perfect day for being out of doors. Armed with sunscreen, mosquito repellant, and binoculars for bird and other wildlife watching, they had come by early to pick up Dervla. Annie was glad. It was good for Dervla to be out, and it was that much more time that she and Tony could spend together with family.

Time was what was needed, Annie thought, to help everyone to feel more comfortable with the situation. She just wished that Gwen would spend some time with Dervla. It was as if she didn't want to get to know her. Was she afraid that she would actually like the woman who was engaged to her son? Perhaps Mary Beth's idea to have a shower for Dervla would help inspire Gwen to be more accepting.

As soon as Dervla had left, Annie went into action. First, she looked through her extra boxes, looking for one that would work to mail the crocheted items, and a second one that would hold the wedding dress. She found one that would work perfectly for a mailer, but she couldn't find a box she thought she could use to safely transport the dress and the accessories. A giant shopping bag would have to do.

After she had sealed and labeled the package for her friend, she headed upstairs with the shopping bag to remove the wedding dress from the mannequin. Having unbuttoned and buttoned the dress twice, she was starting to feel like an expert. The lighting was much brighter that morning than it had been during the storm, so she could see the detail of the handwork.

The quality on the exterior of the dress was apparent. She wondered about the interior. Gram had always told her that, besides the quality of the fabric, the best way to tell the quality of a garment was to check out the seams. Hand-finished seams and hems were the best, she had said.

After she removed it from the mannequin, Annie carried the dress across the room and gently laid it out on the bed so she could examine it more closely. Though the dress was old, she didn't think it had been made before the advent of the sewing machine. Even so, when she inspected the inside, it looked to her as if the dress was completely hand-sewn. It was lined with a lighter-weight fabric, and all of the seams she could see were flat-felled. Another thing Gram had taught her was that her crochet work should look as neat on the wrong side as it did on the right side; someone must have taught this seamstress the same thing. There were no loose threads or frayed edges, as old as it was.

And then she saw them. Sewn to the lining along the side of the waist were not one, but two small labels. One label looked professional—the words were woven into the fabric:

L. & M. Sarto
Custom Dressmakers
Charles Street, Boston
Established 1892

The other label was made of linen. Tiny flowers and leaves had been embroidered, vine-like, around the edges, and in the center, in the same-color pink as the crocheted flowers on the veil, was a name embroidered in an elegant script:

Amanda McKay Grey

Underneath the name, in the same fine embroidery, was a year: 1918.

Annie wasn't sure what this meant. Two labels. Obviously, the dress must have been purchased from the dressmakers named on the woven label, but what did the second label mean? Was the embroidered label just a way of identifying the owner, or did it mean that Amanda Grey was the person who crocheted the trim on the dress and the accessories that made up the wedding ensemble?

She felt a shiver run up her spine as she held the dress in her hands and studied the embroidery on the label. She felt an immediate connection to this woman from the past, a woman with the last name Grey. Seeing the signature written in thread, Annie imagined that it was more than just a name; it was like a message sent across time ... *to whom?* she wondered. Was it a message for a stranger in the future, simply to say, "This was mine," or was she saying, "This is the work of my hands"? Another thought occurred to Annie: Was the embroiderer sending a message to someone special— "this is for you"—a daughter, or a granddaughter, who might someday wear the same dress?

"How did you come to have this dress, Gram?" Annie asked out loud.

There was no answer, only more questions, foremost of which was: Who was Amanda Grey and what was her connection to Captain Grey and Grey Gables? Annie looked again at the pink color that matched the veil flowers and the expertise of the needlework on the label. Something in the way it was done seemed to say to her that the hands that had embroidered the name and date were the same hands that had worked the crocheted details of the dress and the accessories.

*   *   *   *

Annie arrived at Expert Cleaners with plenty of time to spare before the meeting at A Stitch in Time. She had carefully folded the dress and placed it in the shopping bag and added the veil and gloves, placing layers of tissue paper between them and over top to protect them.

The small building that housed the cleaners might have been mistaken for someone's home were it not for the swinging glass door that opened into the drop-off and pick-up area. It was a little blue cottage with a big picture window, in front of which was a flower box full of red geraniums. Of course, the other giveaway was the sign out front—engraved with the business name and a stylized clothing hanger at the top—which hung from a cantilevered cedar post.

She had been in the establishment before, taking in her winter coat and several other items to be dry-cleaned during the time she'd been in Stony Point, but she hadn't noticed that they also specialized in the care and cleaning of antique clothing and other textiles. It was a family business, run by a husband-and-wife team named Kurt and Molly Williams. This morning, the proprietress of the business was standing at the front desk doing some paperwork.

"Hi, Molly!" Annie said as she lifted the shopping bag

onto the counter. "I've brought in an antique wedding dress to be cleaned, and it needs special attention. Mary Beth tells me you're the best for that sort of thing."

Molly smiled at the compliment and said, "Well, let's see what you've got."

After she and Annie had removed the contents of the shopping bag, and Molly had expressed her appreciation of its beauty, Annie showed her the labels she had found inside the dress.

"Ahh, the Misses Sarto," said Molly. "They were sisters—Lucia and Marietta—Kurt and I went to a fashion and textile exhibition in Boston at the Museum of Fine Arts a few years ago that included some custom-made dresses from the late nineteenth and early twentieth centuries. The museum had several dresses that had been made in the sisters' shop. Apparently, they were much in demand because of their very fine workmanship, so quite a few of the dresses they made were preserved. This is in wonderful condition— almost as if it were never worn. Where did you get it?"

Annie explained, once again, how she found the dress in the attic, and her theory that it was Amanda Grey who had added the crochet to the dress, and had made the accessories.

Molly examined the veil and gloves. "These are expertly made. You might be right about the crochet. I may be able to tell you a little more once I've looked over the dress more carefully." As she continued to study the veil, she said, "I think we'll need to try to remove this wire. It might discolor the veil if it becomes wet, or it might rust, which is even worse. I'll have to figure out the best way to do that without doing any damage to the stitching. It looks like a stiffener must have been used on the flowers and leaves around the wreath of the veil to keep them in the proper shape. One of the old ways to stiffen crochet was to use sugar in a solution of water, but I don't think that's the case here. She probably used a starch solution. I'll photograph all the parts to make sure we get everything back the way it should be."

Annie berated herself: "I can't believe I never even thought of taking photos of it! I could have shared them at the Hook and Needle Club meeting. Good grief—I'm totally brainless sometimes. Could you be sure to take a photo of the labels as well?"

Molly laughed. "We all have our lapses at times. Taking photographs before and after cleaning is our standard practice for antiques to make sure we get everything back to the original state—only cleaner, of course. I'll be sure to get a good shot of the labels too. If you're interested in selling the dress, you might contact the museum—I'm sure they'd give you a good price, with the labels intact and the prime condition of it. I'd say at least a thousand; probably more."

Annie was surprised at that, but only said, "Oh, no—I'm lending it to a friend to wear for her wedding."

"Someone here in town?" asked Molly

"No ... well yes, actually—it's Tony Palmers' fiancée, Dervla O'Keefe."

"Oh!—yes, I met her at church on Sunday. She's a beautiful girl. I'll bet this design will really suit her," said Molly.

"It does," said Annie, remembering Dervla's ghostlike descent down the staircase at Grey Gables and the look on

Andrew's face. "It's like it was made for her."

Annie paused and then asked, "About the Sarto sisters ... did the museum have any information about them—like, how long they were in business?"

"Yes, they did have a lot of information about them. I recall them in particular because their story took a rather interesting turn. The younger sister, Marietta, left the shop, after working there several years, when she got married. Lucia continued to run the business quite a while after that, but eventually moved out West—sometime between 1911 and 1914, I think—I'll have to check the exact year with Kurt to see if he remembers. It was a bit of a scandal because she went out to Hollywood to become a costume designer when the movie industry was just taking off out there."

Annie laughed, "I guess that would be a scandalous thing to do according to staid old Boston! Well, that would seem to date the dress a lot earlier than the year that is on the embroidered label."

"Oh yes," said Molly, "this design is much earlier. I'd say it's from right at the end of the Victorian era—definitely before 1900. Nineteen eighteen was the tail end of World War I, and clothing styles changed a lot during the war."

Annie and Molly chatted for a bit about the changes in fashion around that time, until another customer entered the shop. Molly told Annie that the dress should be ready for pickup by Friday. Annie was glad to have someone so knowledgeable taking care of the ensemble. She'd have a lot to tell the other ladies at the Hook and Needle Club meeting.

*   *   *   *

After running a couple more errands, Annie reached A Stitch in Time just a few minutes after eleven. Everyone else was already there—even Alice, who was often running behind schedule. The bell rang as she opened the door, and everyone had looked up when she entered, but besides perfunctory hellos, they all seemed unusually quiet. There was none of the normal chatter about what they were working on or the other things that had been going on in their lives. As she took her usual seat, Annie thought to herself that it was more than just quiet; there was tension in the air.

Mary Beth spoke once Annie was seated. "Annie—glad you're here." She glanced sideways at Gwen as she continued, "I had just mentioned what we had talked about on Sunday—about having a 'hope chest' shower for Dervla." Annie noticed that Gwen didn't look up from her knitting, and her mouth made a grim line. The others seemed to be constrained by Gwen's stony expression. Only Stella seemed the same as ever, knitting needles clicking away. "You've spent more time with her than anyone else—do you think she would like something like that?"

"I think she'd love it," Annie answered. "She has a real appreciation for beautiful things, and I know she only brought one large and one small suitcase on the plane, so I'm pretty sure she would only have her clothing with her. She may have a lot of things in Ireland, but I don't think she had time to organize anything household-wise to ship over. More than anything, I think she would appreciate the opportunity for friendship that a get-together like that would offer."

"What exactly is a 'hope chest'?" asked Peggy, who was

the youngest of the group and inclined to be more interested in current styles and customs.

Though Kate was not that much older than Peggy, she
had a soft spot for the way things were done in the past,
so she was the one who answered, "Back in the day, most
young girls had a hope chest. It was a present she received
when she turned twelve or thirteen, and the idea was that
she would spend the next few years filling it with things she
would use to set up household when she got married. Often,
the chest itself was a box made of cedar, and the girl would
collect or make things for her trousseau, which included
articles for setting up household—a linen tablecloth and
napkins, lacy curtains, white cotton dishtowels, crocheted
doilies, embroidered pillowcases—all kinds of things. Also,
she might make things for her honeymoon like a special
dress, lingerie, and accessories—gloves, scarves. She might
purchase things like silver serving spoons, a fancy vanity set
with a comb, brush, and handheld mirror ..."

"Wow!" said Peggy, interrupting the flow of Kate's list,
"how do you know so much about it?"

"I just think it's such a lovely custom, and I remember
my grandmother's cedar chest," replied Kate. "She kept all
her special remembrances in it, and sometimes she would
take out some of the items to show me. Besides keeping old
pictures, she still had a stitch sampler she'd made when
she was a teenager, and pressed flowers she had saved from
bouquets that Grandpa had given her ... I loved seeing what
she'd saved. And though a girl can 'hope' for a lot more besides marriage these days, she still needs to have things to
start with when she's on her own. I started a hope chest for

Vanessa, actually. I couldn't afford a real cedar chest, but I bought a footlocker for a reasonable price, and she and I lined it with a pretty, self-adhesive shelf-liner paper. We painted the outside a nice royal blue color. I made a couple of sachets with cedar chips to put inside to give it that great smell—it's almost like having the real thing when you open the lid and the aroma wafts out. At least it will do until I can get her the real thing."

"That sounds really neat," said Peggy. "I could do something like that for Emily when she gets older."

"I have my old hope chest," said Stella. "It once belonged to my great-grandmother. She brought it over with her when she came to this country. It became mine when my mother died when I was just a child. I keep my own special treasures next to the ones that belonged to them, like your grandmother did, Kate."

"So, that's the sort of thing I was thinking of for Dervla," said Mary Beth. "We don't have to do anything grand— just simple items with small touches to make them special and personal, but things that she can use. Perhaps in time they will be as special to her or her daughters as Stella's are to her." Mary Beth purposely looked at Gwen and asked, "What do you think, Gwen?"

Gwen didn't say anything at first, but she almost looked angry. Finally she began to speak, "It's very kind of you all to want to do this, but I really wouldn't want you to waste your time. I don't think there will be a wedding. This engagement is just something Tony rushed into without thinking. I'm sure once he's had a chance to reconsider, he's going to change his mind. I don't doubt that she's a nice girl. She's certainly pretty enough, and we know how that can turn a young man's head. But I just don't think he will go through with it. He has his whole life ahead of him, and it wouldn't be right for him to be tied down to a girl that he's going to come to realize isn't right for him. His father and I are trying to talk some sense into him, and it won't be long before he finally listens and sends her back home to Ireland."

Annie's mouth had fallen open in amazement as she listened to Gwen. Instead of getting used to the idea of a new daughter-in-law, it seemed that Gwen's hesitancy to accept Dervla had become determination to get her out of Tony's life. Annie wasn't the only one who was surprised at the vehemence of Gwen's comments. The other ladies in the circle looked equally stunned, except Stella, who had stopped knitting and was looking at Gwen steadily. Gwen looked at the others and read their expressions.

"Do whatever you want," said Gwen. "I just don't want to have anything to do with encouraging that girl to stay here. He'll get over her soon enough." And with that, Gwen put away her knitting in her carry-along bag and stood up. "I'm meeting John for lunch, so I have to leave early today." Without another word, she walked out the door.

After a few moments, looking at Mary Beth and whispering as if she thought Gwen might hear her, Peggy said, "What do we do now?"

"As soon as I brought it up, it seemed like the temperature in the room dropped ten degrees, but I had no idea that she was so opposed to the marriage," said Mary Beth. "I thought she was just still having trouble getting used to the idea. I think we're going to have to forget about the shower.

Gwen's our friend, and one of our group—we can't just go ahead with something that she is so opposed to."

Alice spoke up. "I'm sorry, but I disagree. Is that all we're here for—closing ranks when one of us says the word? If we'd done that, Annie wouldn't be part of the group now—as I recall there was a bit of reluctance to let her join us when she first arrived, not naming any names … Stella."

Stella gave Alice a wry look. "That was a misunderstanding … and a result, perhaps, of my natural inclination to be … somewhat stubborn. I have to admit that I was, as you say, reluctant at first, but everything worked out in the end."

"Exactly," said Alice, "but not because we gave in to your doubts. I say we go ahead with the shower. I've spent some time with Dervla, too, and I like her. I don't care if she marries Tony Palmer or not, though I personally don't doubt for a moment that they love each other. She's a stranger here, and I want to be a friend to her."

Mary Beth sighed. "I guess we can put it to a vote. We have to count Gwen as a 'no' I think. … All those in favor of having a shower for Dervla raise your hand."

Annie, Alice, and Kate all raised their hands. Annie was surprised when Stella joined them. Mary Beth and Peggy seemed surprised too. Slowly, Peggy raised her hand as well.

"It looks like the vote is for having the shower," said Mary Beth. "Perhaps I can talk to Gwen, and explain that we just want to show Dervla some friendship—as a stranger in Stony Point. I hope it doesn't cause a rift that can't be repaired."

— 11 —

The ladies of the Hook and Needle Club, minus Gwendolyn, decided that the "hope chest" shower for Dervla should be a surprise, so it was arranged that it would be held at the carriage house, where Alice lived, next door to Grey Gables. They gave themselves a little less than two weeks to work on their projects, setting the time and date for two o'clock in the afternoon the second Saturday after their meeting. Mary Beth would close A Stitch in Time early that day, and Peggy thought she could get the afternoon off from The Cup & Saucer.

They agreed that each of them would bring some sort of finger food—sweet or savory, and Alice said she would provide table service and drinks. At first they decided they were going to forego any of the usual party games that are the common thing at showers, but Alice recommended that they played one that would help them all get to know Dervla a bit better. She said she would make copies of a list of ten or fifteen questions that inquired about Dervla's favorites—her favorite color, song or type of music, type of pet, food, season, time of day, hobby, flower, etc. Dervla would write down her answers, and the others would write down answers, trying to guess how Dervla had answered them. Alice said she would supply a "prize" for the person who answered the most questions the same as Dervla. Though none of them really knew her that well, just the process of guessing, and then comparing them with Dervla's answers, would provide a little insight into her personality.

Peggy and Kate wanted to bring along their daughters, and Kate thought that Vanessa would want to invite her best friend Mackenzie, since Vanessa had talked nonstop about Ireland since meeting Dervla. Both teens had learned to crochet the previous summer, and Kate said she would get them to work on some easy projects—dishcloths or hot pads—so that they could present Dervla with homemade gifts as well. Peggy said that Emily had received a pot-holder loom for her last birthday, and though her daughter was only a first-grader, Peggy thought she would be proud to be able to give Dervla something she had made herself.

It was also decided they would send invitations to Tony's sister, Meredith, and his sister-in-law, Sandra. Sandra was in Portland, so there was really no good reason that she couldn't come, but Annie had her doubts that she would show up. She wished that Meredith lived closer, or that they could arrange to have the shower while she was still in town, but she and Frank and the kids were heading back to North Carolina on Friday. Perhaps Meredith would send a gift; there should be someone or something at the shower to represent the Palmer family, and Meredith had proved that she was willing to be a friend to Dervla. Annie was certain that Gwen wouldn't show up, even though Mary Beth was going to try to talk her into it.

The first forty minutes of the hour-long meeting had been spent planning the shower, and when they had finalized their plans, Annie decided to tell the others about discovering the labels in the wedding dress, and her theory that it was Amanda Grey who had worked the crocheted parts. She also told them what Molly Williams had said about the dressmakers. She decided not to mention that she had offered the dress to Dervla for her wedding.

"I can't wait to see this dress," said Kate, "especially the crocheted parts."

"Maybe we can arrange something when I get it back from the cleaners," said Annie. "The labels make it even more interesting, I think. I wondered if you had ever heard of Amanda McKay Grey, Stella," said Annie.

"I don't recall that name," said Stella. "The only person named Grey who lived in Stony Point that I've ever known of was Captain Grey, but McKay is a well-known name in Boston. Maybe she was a sister-in-law or something."

"Then how did it get to Grey Gables?" asked Alice. "Are you sure Captain Grey never married?"

"I didn't say that he *hadn't* married," said Stella, "only that when I knew of him, he was alone. I guess he would have been older than I am now when he died, so he lived the major portion of his life before I was even born."

"Did you ever check at the library to see if you can find any information on him there, Annie?" asked Mary Beth.

"No—I haven't had a chance yet," said Annie. She thought of Andrew Gareth, whom she was certain had a wealth of information, if only she could get him to share some of it. She didn't mention him to the others. No one, besides Alice, had asked yet, so she assumed that news about the painter hadn't leaked out yet—otherwise Peggy, at the very least, would have been seeking information about him.

The hour had passed. Peggy had to return to work at the diner, and a tour bus had unloaded its passengers on Main Street, so Mary Beth and Kate were suddenly busy with a crowd of shoppers. Stella remained in her chair and continued to knit. Annie and Alice both decided to look around the shop a bit.

Annie wanted to browse through the pattern books to see if she could find something suitable for Dervla's shower. She knew that she could crochet a few dishcloths and hot pads with cotton yarn in no time flat, but since the less-experienced teens were going to provide those, she'd thought she'd like to make something for Dervla that would be more of a keepsake than entirely practical. The question was, what could she make that was special but could be finished quickly? She couldn't seem to find anything that would suit her criteria. There were a couple of patterns she really liked, but she knew from just looking at the instructions that she could never complete either one in the time allotted. She decided she would look through her grandmother's collection of crochet books in the library and see if she could find something appropriate.

Annie and Alice left A Stitch in Time at the same time, so Annie asked Alice if she wanted to have lunch with her at The Cup & Saucer. Alice answered that she would have liked to, but she had to make a presentation at a Devine Décor party that afternoon, and didn't have the time.

"Why don't you come over for dinner this evening?" asked Annie. "I can tell you about Andrew's visit yesterday."

"That would be great!" said Alice. "What can I bring?"

"Nothing—I'll whip up something fabulous."

"I would expect nothing less," said Alice, trying to maintain a straight face. "I'm thinking you could serve baked filet of sole with Lobster Newburg sauce, over a bed of rice pilaf with a nice watercress/Boston lettuce salad on the side, and flambéed pears and frozen gelato served with espresso for desert. Can you handle that?"

"Of course. I may have to substitute a can of tuna for the filet of sole, and a can of cream of chicken soup for the sauce, but I'm sure I have a box of Rice-A-Roni. We can try to light a can of fruit cocktail on fire, but it may not be quite the same."

"On second thought, I'll just let you choose the menu tonight," said Alice.

"A wise choice," said Annie, laughing. "I'll see you later—come on over as soon as you get home."

*   *   *   *

When Annie finally finished her errands, the afternoon had flown away. Her last stop was Magruder's Groceries, where, along with the other things she already had on her list, she picked up green-leaf lettuce and cucumber for a salad, a container of lemon sorbet for dessert, and for the main course, fresh cod, which she would bake and serve with homemade lemon-butter sauce. She planned to prepare rice pilaf from scratch, just to surprise Alice. The menu might not include Lobster Newburg, but she was sure it would be a good meal.

Shortly after Annie returned to Grey Gables, Tony and Dervla returned from their hiking expedition. Both their complexions reflected the hours they had spent out in the sun, despite their use of sunscreen. Dervla's skin was naturally fair and tended toward freckles, and her nose had gotten quite red; it would surely be peeling in a couple of days. They'd had a wonderful time hiking through the natural beauty of Maine.

Seeing them together, laughing as they described the day's activities and just being gloriously happy in each other's company, Annie unwillingly remembered Gwen's harsh comments at the Hook and Needle Club meeting that morning. The contrast between Gwen's hardened expression and the look of bliss on the faces of the young couple was like night and day. She hated to think that Gwen's attitude might squelch their chance to share that happiness throughout their lives.

Meredith and Frank and their children had gone on to Wedgwood, where the plan was that the adults would get ready to go out that evening with Tony and Dervla and leave the grandkids with Gwen and John. After visiting with Annie for a bit, Tony left to walk over to Wedgwood to get a shower and change clothes. Dervla went upstairs to do the same.

Annie decided to wait until the next day to tell Dervla what she'd learned about the wedding dress. Tony was leaving in the morning to drive down to Massachusetts for a few days. He still had an apartment in Cambridge, and had a couple of job interviews to go to in Boston, so there would be plenty of time to tell Dervla all the details after he was gone. She was thinking that she'd have to figure out a way to work on her project without Dervla seeing it. Of course, she hadn't figured out what it was going to be yet. *One bridge at a time*, she thought.

Alice arrived while Dervla was upstairs. She helped herself to a tall glass of lemonade and sat at the kitchen table while Annie prepared dinner. Annie told Alice that she had offered the dress to Dervla for the wedding, and that Dervla had tried it on and it was a perfect fit. They also discussed the labels on the dress, and Annie's idea that Amanda Grey was responsible for all of the crochet.

"So, is there any way to prove that the crochet is newer than the dress?" asked Alice. "Sort of a carbon dating for fibers?"

Annie laughed. "I don't think there is for something so recent," she said. "That is, unless you could determine age of the crochet thread by the process by which it was made, or by the content, say if it contained particular manmade fibers ... but then you'd have to be able to tell the exact age of the wedding-dress cloth too. It's a moot point anyway. I don't think there was much use of the new man-made fibers in clothing until the 1930s. There must be another way."

At that moment, Dervla entered the kitchen looking lovely in an empire-waist dress with swirling, mottled ocean blue fabric reaching down to her ankles. Annie didn't think she had seen Dervla looking so happy since she had met her, only four days ago. Funny; it seemed to Annie that she had known Dervla for years. It was uncanny the effect that the girl had on people. *Well, on certain people,* she thought. For just a moment, the shocked look on Andrew's face when he saw Dervla in the wedding dress flashed in Annie's mind, but her thoughts moved on quickly to Gwen's stern expression at the Hook and Needle Club meeting. She really couldn't understand the disliking that Gwen and John had taken to Dervla. But then, as far as Annie could tell, they hadn't really even tried to get to know her. She remembered the effect Gwen's frown and severe words had on her friends at the Hook and Needle Club meeting. She could imagine the effect that same attitude would have on a stranger, especially a young girl wanting to make a good impression. *Oh, I wish I could make Gwen see what she's doing*, thought Annie.

Dervla and Alice conversed while Annie continued to work on dinner. Soon the doorbell sounded. Assuming that it was Tony, Dervla wished Annie a good evening, and Alice saw the young couple off at the front door.

When Alice returned, she commented on the change in Dervla's demeanor after a day of outdoor activity and fun with Tony and his sister's family. "That girl is just a delight. I'd take her for my daughter-in-law any day of the week."

"So would I. Pity neither one of us has a son," said Annie with a smile. "But then I do think that she and Tony are a good match—I just wish Gwen could see that."

"She will someday," said Alice. "At least, I hope she does. I hate to think that those two might not end up together, or that Tony and his parents might end up estranged because of this. It would be a real shame."

Annie asked Alice to set the table in the dining room for a change—instead of eating in the kitchen—and when dinner was ready they both sat down to enjoy a leisurely meal. Annie told Alice about Andrew Gareth's visit during the storm, including his reactions to Dervla in the wedding dress and to the initials on the hatbox.

"That's rather bizarre," said Alice. "I need to meet this guy. Are you sure he's on the up and up?"

"Yes, Alice, I'm sure he is. I told you about seeing that program on TV and going to his exhibit in Texas."

"Yes," said Alice, "but are you sure it's really him? Did you ask for ID?"

"No, I didn't ask for ID," said Annie, "but I'm sure it's really him. First of all, I'm sure that Ian has checked him out. And second, I just know it—by the way he talks about his work, and you should have seen the drawing he was working on in the library. It was amazing what he did, and so quickly."

"Well, a lot of people can draw, Annie. I think you should make sure he's who he says he is," said Alice.

"What do you want me to do? Steal his wallet?" asked Annie.

"It's a thought," kidded Alice. Then she said in a serious tone, "Just be careful, Annie. Sometimes you're just too trusting."

When they had finished dinner, they cleared away the dishes and settled in the living room to talk about their plans for Dervla's hope-chest shower.

"I've been working on embroidering some tea towels," said Alice, "but I'm not sure they're what I want to give her. Something with an Irish theme might be nicer. There's an Irish symbol, called a *claddagh*. It has a heart that stands for love in the center, with a crown on top that stands for fidelity, or loyalty; there are two hands, one on each side, holding the heart, and those stand for friendship. It's a symbol that's often used on wedding rings. I was thinking I could make a runner or a table topper—not too large—out of linen, and embroider that symbol in each corner, maybe with some tracery work on either side. Or I could place the claddagh symbol in the center and just the tracery work in the corners, sort of like fancy brackets. I'm not sure what to do yet."

"That sounds fabulous, Alice," said Annie. "You could do what Gram always did, draw it out on paper both ways and then color it in to get a sense of how it's going to look. Then you can choose what you like the best before you invest all the time and materials in the actual embroidery. I have some graph paper in the library, and colored pencils and markers too. And I'm pretty sure Gram has a book about all kinds of symbols—maybe we can find that one. Let's go have a look."

Annie and Alice went to the library, and while Annie was retrieving the drawing materials from her grandmother's desk, Alice scanned book titles, looking for one that might have the symbol she had described.

"Here it is," said Alice, "or I should say, here they are … she has several on signs and symbols." Alice pulled three large-size books off the shelf. Looking at the covers, she said, "This one says it's about Christian symbology, and this one is called … *Semiotics: The Philosophy of Symbols*. That sounds a little too deep for me." She laid down the first two books and flipped through the third one. "This is more like it—it's full of drawings and seems to be categorized according to culture. Let's see—there's a section on Assyrian symbols, and Egyptian, Greek, … Roman, … Germanic, Scandinavian, … here we are! Celtic symbols, including a four-leaf clover, Celtic knot work, and … it's here! The claddagh ring! This is perfect!"

Alice sat down at Betsy Holden's desk to begin to plot out her ideas on paper. While Alice was working, Annie thought she would try to figure out what she was going to make for Dervla by looking through her grandmother's collection of crochet pattern books. Then the flower guide caught her eye. There was still the matter of the unidentified flower on the hatbox lid. She pulled the flower guide and the book next to it off the shelf, the one she had almost looked at the day before—*The Language of Flowers.*

She flipped through it to see what it was like. The book was old. Gram must have bought it from a library sale or something—Annie didn't remember it being in the library during the summers of her youth. There were no photographs inside, but instead beautifully drawn illustrations of all kinds of flowers, in all stages of their growth—from the bud just peeking out of the calyx, to the flower in full bloom, and in some cases, the drooping flower as the petals began to drop off. Beside each illustration was the Latin name of the flower, along with whatever common names were given to it. Underneath the name were meanings associated with the individual flowers.

"What have you got there?" asked Alice, looking up from her paper.

"It's a book about flowers and what they mean—I noticed it the other day when I was in here with Andrew. It has beautiful illustrations."

Annie turned the pages back to the introduction at the front of the book and read aloud, "Going back as far as the Egyptians, Greeks, and Romans in ancient times, certain meanings were assigned to individual types of flowers, as well as herbs and other types of greenery that were valued for their appearance and the scents that they emitted. People in ancient cultures made bouquets, wreaths, and garlands, and used them in their rites of passage—birth, coming of age, marriage, and death. Flower symbols were woven into mythologies and became associated with particular meanings."

"That's interesting," said Alice, as she continued to work on her cross-stitch graph.

Annie read silently through several pages about the multiple layers of meaning that continued to be added to flowers and various plants by people in the Middle Ages and during the Renaissance, and then about changes that occurred after the discovery of the New World with the new varieties of plants found there. Eventually she came to a section about the meaning of flowers in the Victorian age. After reading through the section, an idea occurred to her.

"Alice, listen to this," said Annie; from the book, she read aloud: "'The Victorians rediscovered the ancient language of flowers, and it became popular to send secret messages to one's sweetheart by means of a bouquet.' You know that hand-painted bouquet on the hatbox—what if it's more than just a pretty picture?"

"You mean you think someone might have been trying to send an illicit love message with a hatbox?" asked Alice. Answering her own question, she said, "Hmm. I don't know—it's an intriguing idea."

"Well, as pretty as it is, it is an unusual combination of flowers for a bouquet, don't you think?" asked Annie.

"I've only seen it the one time—I can't exactly remember the flowers that were on it," said Alice.

"I'm going to go get the box and bring it down. I'll be right back," Annie said. She went upstairs to retrieve the now-empty hatbox and brought it back to the library and sat it on her grandfather's desk.

"So now what?" asked Alice. She laid down the marker she had been using to add color to her drawing, stood up and walked over to stand beside Annie to look at the painting on the hatbox.

"Now we're going to figure out what this last flower on the hatbox is," Annie replied. "I have Gram's old flower guide," she said as she picked up the book from where she had laid it, "and then we can use *The Language of Flowers* book to see what each flower means."

Looking at the hatbox, Annie and Alice took note of the unidentified flower. It had clumps of small pink petals and long spindly things that stuck out below the petals. They looked through the flower guide until they found a picture that resembled it. Annie read out loud: "*Cleome hassleriana*, commonly known as the spider flower, so-called because of the long, thin seedpods that project from under the petals. An annual plant with five-point leaves and compound flowers, which may be purple, pink, or white."

"The spider flower," said Alice, "ick—that doesn't sound like it could mean anything too pleasing."

Putting aside the flower guide, Annie sat down at her grandfather's desk, opened the side drawer, and got out a medium-size notebook with lined paper and a pen. In the form of a list, she began writing down all the varieties of plants that had been painted on the hatbox, beginning with the greenery, and then the flowers, placing the spider flower at the bottom of the column.

While Annie wrote, Alice moved the other desk chair next to her. Alice grabbed *The Language of Flowers* book and sat down to begin the task of looking up the first plant. "According to the book," said Alice, "the wreath of ivy around the edge symbolizes friendship, fidelity, and marriage." Annie wrote down "friendship, fidelity, and marriage" next to "Ivy."

Second on the list was "Fern"—the book said it symbolized sincerity; Annie wrote "sincerity" in the second column. Alice and Annie continued on to the next word on the list. Both had expected the four-leaf clover to mean "good luck," but were surprised when the book said it meant "be mine."

Then they began to look up the flowers. The book informed them that pansies "remind the recipient to think of the one who sent the flowers, and to tell her that she occupies his thoughts." They guessed it was assumed by the author that the sender would be a man, and the recipient a woman. Violets were said to express "faithful love."

There were just three more flowers on the list. The book said that the meaning of the primrose was "I can't live without you," and that Jacob's ladder meant "come down to me." Finally, they found the last flower on the list, the spider flower. When Annie saw the meaning, she involuntarily caught her breath. The words on the page said the spider flower was given as a secret message that meant, "elope with me."

Alice and Annie looked at each other, speechless for a moment. Then, starting at the top, Annie read aloud the litany of meanings again as she had written them down: "Friendship, fidelity, and marriage; sincerity; 'be mine'; 'think of me as I think of you'; faithful love; 'I can't live without you'; 'come down to me'; 'elope with me.'"

"These had to have been chosen on purpose," said Alice. "There's no way this could be an accident."

Annie answered, "I agree. I think that this P.R.G. person painted the hatbox lid ... and then gave it to ... Amanda, maybe? I'm just remembering the look on Andrew's face when I pointed out the letters on the box. I think he knows who P.R.G. is. But why keep it a secret? Presumably, these people have been gone for decades; what could it matter? Andrew keeps saying how interested he is in Grey Gables and Captain Grey, but he tells me nothing. I think I'll make a trip to the library tomorrow and see what I can find out myself about Captain Grey, and Amanda Grey too. There's bound to be something in the archives about the residents of Stony Point around that time. If all else fails, I'll just confront Andrew and ask him what he knows."

⌐ 12 ⌐

Annie spent a fitful night trying to put all the pieces together from what she had learned so far about the wedding dress with its two labels, and the hatbox with its secret message. She felt certain that Andrew Gareth knew more than he was telling. Annie wasn't by nature a confrontational person, but she was persistent when it came to finding out the truth. Truth was important to her, and in her experience it was always better for everyone involved to know the truth. The thing was, as far as she knew, everyone involved in this mystery was dead and gone, and had been for decades. It could make no difference to them now.

There were just too many gaps in her knowledge to come to any definite conclusions. She hoped she could gather some more facts through some research at the library. *Andrew Gareth isn't the only one who knows his way around a microfiche machine!* she told herself.

After they'd had breakfast, Annie and Dervla talked about Tony's trip to Boston and the jobs for which he would be interviewing. It had been his intention to leave very early that morning, so he and Dervla had said their goodbyes when he dropped her off at Grey Gables the night before. He wouldn't be heading back to Stony Point until next Monday, after an early-morning interview, and Dervla would have some time on her hands until he returned. Annie offered to drive her to town so she could do some shopping, but before they could decide what exactly to do, the phone and the doorbell rang at the very same time.

Annie laughed. "Dervla, if you would see who's at the front door, I'll answer the phone!"

Annie picked up the receiver in the living room; it was Molly Williams, from Expert Cleaners, on the phone. "Hi Molly," said Annie, "is the dress already finished?"

"No—afraid not," said Molly. "Remember that I told you that I needed to remove the wire from the veil?"

"Yes." said Annie, "Is it all right? I hope it's not damaged."

"No, it isn't that. It's just that I found something … unexpected. Do you think you would have time to come into the shop today? I think it's better that you see it, than for me to try to describe it to you," said Molly.

"Well, now you have piqued my curiosity! I'll be there shortly."

Annie rang off, and went to see who had come to the front door, but no one was in the entry, including Dervla. Annie opened the door and looked outside to see Dervla and Andrew standing side by side on the front lawn, several yards away from Grey Gables. Andrew had set up an easel, and next to the easel was a small folding table, which at the moment held the vinyl-sided bag he'd brought with him the day of the storm. She thought he must carry his art supplies with him everywhere, so if inspiration or opportunity struck, he'd be prepared. At that moment, both he and Dervla were looking at the house, and he seemed to be describing something to her using expressive hand gestures. When he saw Annie at the door, he waved to her to come outside too.

Annie walked down the porch steps and across the lawn to join them. "Good morning, Annie!" said Andrew. "I was just asking a favor of Dervla, and I have one to ask of you as well. It is my plan to do a proper portrait of Grey Gables, but I'd also like to include it in the background of another painting—a portrait of a lady in the wedding dress you found in the attic, and I've asked Dervla to be my model— I'd pay her, of course." Dervla started to speak, but Andrew interrupted, "You don't need to make that decision yet. Hear me out first."

Speaking to Annie, he said, "Seeing her in that wedding dress gave me the idea that a portrait like that could add another layer of meaning to the story I'm trying to tell through my paintings about Stony Point. You see, Grey Gables was built as a wedding present from Zacharias Grey to Amanda, his bride-to-be. Construction was begun in 1895, and they were married in 1896. By the time they returned from their honeymoon in Europe, the house was completed."

"I see ... I think," said Annie. "You'd like to paint Dervla wearing the wedding ensemble, and Grey Gables would be in the background—over her shoulder or something— right?"

"Exactly," said Andrew.

"Wait. ... Did you just say that a woman named Amanda was married to Captain Grey?" asked Annie.

"Yes, that's right. Amanda McKay. She was several years younger than he was. Her family was in the shipping business too. Quite wealthy. It was a good match for him," said Andrew.

"Why hadn't Stella heard of her?" asked Annie. "She said Captain Grey lived alone."

"I'm sure that by the time your friend knew of him, he was alone. Amanda died in the flu epidemic of 1918," replied Andrew.

"She died ... in 1918?" said Annie. In her mind's eye she saw the embroidered signature and date she had found inside the wedding dress: *Amanda McKay Grey ... 1918*. Was that embroidery the last needlework she ever did?

Andrew looked at Annie's expression and read that she knew something more. "What is it, Annie? Have you heard of Amanda Grey somewhere else?"

"Yes," said Annie. Then she told Andrew and Dervla about finding the labels in the dress the previous day, and what she had learned from Molly Williams about the dressmakers when she took the ensemble to have it cleaned.

Looking at Andrew's expression, Annie thought that he looked like wheels were turning in his head, putting two and two together and coming up with ... what? He said nothing. *He knows something more*, Annie thought, *but he's not telling*. There was no way to force him to reveal more than he was willing to.

"At any rate," said Annie, "it will have to wait. I'm willing that you should use the dress for the painting, but it won't be ready until Friday."

"Then we could begin Saturday morning, if the weather cooperates, and if Dervla is willing," said Andrew, looking at her hopefully.

Dervla seemed to consider his offer, and looked at Annie, "What do you think, Annie? Shall I pose for his painting?"

"Well, of course it's your decision, but I think it would be wonderful, and a fitting tribute to both Grey Gables and to Amanda Grey."

"Then it's settled," said Dervla, taking Andrew's hand to shake on the agreement. "I'll be ready bright and early Saturday morning."

"Perfect," said Andrew.

Annie had noted before that although Andrew was a pleasant man who smiled easily, the distant expression in his eyes usually gave her the feeling that he wasn't entirely engaged in the moment—that he was always thinking of more and other things. This time, as he looked down into Dervla's beautiful upturned face, the smile on his face most definitely did reach into his eyes. She hoped that she had given Dervla the right advice.

*   *   *   *

Later that morning, Annie dropped Dervla downtown so that she could pick up a few things that she needed while Annie went to Expert Cleaners to find out what Molly had discovered when removing the wire from the veil. As soon as she entered the little blue cottage, Molly came into the front room to greet her.

"Hi, Annie! Thanks for coming over so quickly. Come on around the counter and follow me to the back so I can show you what I found."

Annie followed Molly into the processing area behind the front room. She could hear the muffled whirring sounds of the dry-cleaning machines from an adjacent room. The processing area was full of racks of clothing—some were covered with clear plastic bags, some that looked like they were waiting to be cleaned, and some looked to be waiting to be steam-pressed. It was hot in the room, even though it was air-conditioned, and it smelled of dry-cleaning chemicals. Annie felt a dampness spring up on her forehead and chin, but Molly seemed to be used to it.

"I started on your wedding ensemble late yesterday afternoon," said Molly as they walked. "I wanted to be sure there was plenty of time for everything to air-dry. The trailing part of the veil was attached to the inside of the flower wreath, and I needed to detach it before I could get the wire out. That worked fine—you see the wreath drying over there."

Molly pointed to a large, long worktable. On the table, the wreath had been placed on the head of a bust—like one might see in a department store to display hats or wigs—to shape it properly while it dried. Next to it on the table, the long veil was laid out over a light green-color foam mat, with the corners and other strategic points pinned down into the foam.

"This is what I wanted you to see," said Molly. "At the top, where it was attached to the wreath, the veil had been folded over a few times, and this is what I saw when I unfolded it."

Annie looked down at the veil. Once again, she appreciated the fine detail of the filet crochet ... there were scattered motifs of flowers and birds, and tiny butterflies she hadn't noticed before. Then her attention moved to the area that Molly indicated. There were words across the top rows

of the veil, written in the blocks and meshes that made up
the technique of filet crochet:

Dear Father in Heaven, please hear my prayer:
Be with my daughter, keep her in Thy care,
Bless her and watch her through all of her days,
Help us to trust Your mysterious ways.

"Oh my," said Annie, struck nearly speechless for the
moment by the sentiment of the prayer—a woman's prayer
for her daughter, hidden from the human eye for all that
time, but always there. Annie had heard of things like prayer
quilts and prayer shawls, where the maker said a prayer for
the intended recipient with each stitch she made, but she'd
never seen something like this, with the very words of the
prayer embedded in the work itself.

Annie remembered what Andrew had told her earlier
that day—that Amanda McKay had married Zacharias Grey.
Now she was sure that the dress had been Amanda McKay's
wedding gown, and that it had to be that Amanda had added all of the crocheted trim to it, not when she originally
wore it in 1896, but in 1918, for her daughter, shortly before Amanda died. Andrew had said nothing about children;
maybe he didn't know there had been a daughter.

Once again, Annie wondered why the dress had been in
her grandmother's attic. Even though she now knew what
the connection had been between the wedding dress and
Grey Gables, it didn't explain why it was still there if the
daughter had been married in it. Or had she? Perhaps she
died in the epidemic as well, and her father couldn't deal

with it. If he had just left it in the house, maybe Annie's grandmother had found it and eventually placed it on the mannequin for Annie to find—as she had left so many other things in that attic. Annie often felt that the mysteries she'd been involved in since she moved to Grey Gables were not accidents. There was some unseen hand, leading her … "divine providence" her grandmother would have said. *There is something in that,* thought Annie.

Then she remembered the hatbox and the secret message of the painted flowers on the lid—"elope with me." What a strange thing for Amanda to keep the crocheted wedding accessories in. Or did she not know there was a message? Perhaps her daughter eloped with P.R.G. and never used the dress and the accessories her mother had made just for her. Only yesterday Annie guessed that it might have been Amanda who eloped with the painter of the bouquet. She'd been wrong about that, but she wished there was some way she could find out who had painted the hatbox— and how the Greys were connected to it. If only Andrew would be more forthcoming about what he had discovered in his research.

Molly spoke, interrupting Annie's thoughts, "The thing is, I wanted you to see this before I reattach the veil to the wreath—that is, if you still want me to do that."

Part of Annie wanted to leave it separate, so that she could show the ladies at the Hook and Needle Club if nothing else, but then it seemed wrong not to put it back the way Amanda had originally sewn it together. Then she had an idea. "I think we should try to put it back just the way it was," said Annie, "but, if you would, if you have a dark-color cloth somewhere, when the veil is dry, lay it on that cloth and take a picture of the veil from overhead, so it can be read, and so that we have record of it. How does that sound?"

"That sounds like a good idea to me," said Molly. "I agree that it's better to keep it in the original condition, but it will be good to have a record of the entire thing. I can put all of the photos I've taken on a disk for you, so you can view them on your computer, or print them out if you wish.

"That's perfect!" said Annie. "Thanks for calling me over to see this, Molly. Knowing that a message is there, even though it's hidden away, makes the entire ensemble all the more special. I appreciate how meticulous you've been in taking care of it."

Annie and Dervla had arranged that they would meet at A Stitch in Time at about eleven thirty. Annie walked the short distance from Expert Cleaners to look around the store before Dervla showed up. Mary Beth and Kate said hello, but were both occupied, each helping customers find the perfect yarn or fabric or pattern, as was required. It was good to see so many people in the shop. Tourists who spent time in Stony Point seemed to like to roam through the selection of yarns and fabrics as much as the locals. Annie thought it was partly because of the ambiance of the store— just stepping inside inspired her to be more creative and gave her the desire to try new things with her needlework. She thought others must be similarly inspired.

Soon, the bell on the door jingled, and Dervla stepped inside. She was a bit early as well. At her side she carried a large cloth tote bag in a bright floral pattern, its straps looped over her shoulder. Seeing Annie she said, "Hi, Annie! This is the first time I've been in this store. It's wonderful. Do you mind if I look around a little before we go home?"

"Not at all," replied Annie. "There are still a few things I want to check out. Even though I come here every week, it seems like there's always something new to see. Where did you find that tote? It's cute."

"I bought it over at Malone's Hardware. They had a large display, and I thought it would be good to use to carry my purchases, so I don't have to collect a lot of plastic bags."

"Good idea!" said Annie.

Then Dervla said, "Since we're here, remember we had talked about making a petticoat to go under the wedding dress? Could you help me find a pattern and choose some material? I'd like to try to make one myself."

"Another good idea," said Annie, smiling. "I'd be glad to help. We can set up Gram's sewing machine in one of the other bedrooms. I think the first thing to do is to see if we can find a pattern. Then we can check out fabric and any notions you'll need after we have the pattern in hand."

Annie and Dervla spent the next half hour doing just that. They ended up looking in the ladies' costume section of one of the pattern books to find a style that would work to be worn under the wedding dress. Besides a pattern for a full-length petticoat, included with it were patterns for a camisole and old-time bloomers. Dervla and Annie laughed at the thought of wearing bloomers, but both agreed that the picture of them on the envelope, that showed the underclothes on models, was actually kind of cute.

The petticoat pattern called for seven and a quarter

yards of fabric, along with ribbon and lace edging, and six buttons. Dervla chose white batiste, which was lightweight and soft to the touch, pale pink ribbon that matched the color of the flowers on the veil, white crochet lace that looked like it had shells along the edge, and flat white buttons for the back opening. Annie was sure that she had plenty of white thread at home.

Annie was pleased that she could help Dervla with her sewing project, but she thought how much better it would have been if Gwen would have been the one helping Dervla, forming the bond that occurs when an older woman helps a younger one learn a new skill. She was glad to be there for Dervla. She felt sorry for Gwen—she was missing an opportunity that wouldn't come again.

After Dervla had made her purchases and tucked them into her new tote, she and Annie decided to head next door to The Cup & Saucer for lunch. They had chosen the busiest time of day, but hoped they could find a table. When they entered the diner it appeared that every table was occupied, but as luck would have it, Ian Butler was sitting in a booth and waved them over. Sitting across from him was Andrew Gareth.

"Won't you ladies join us?" Ian asked.

As Annie sat down next to Ian, and Dervla slipped into the seat next to Andrew, Annie said, "You'd think after all this time, I'd know better than to come to The Cup & Saucer at this hour when it's always packed full of customers. Thanks for sharing your table ... again! I don't know how many times you've saved me from imminent starvation, Ian."

Ian laughed and said, "Happy to be of help. We just

placed our orders, but I'll try to get Peggy's attention next time she breezes through."

"I'm not worried about it," said Annie. "Peggy's usually pretty good at spotting newcomers. In fact, there isn't much that girl does miss—she's great at noticing every detail. She'd make a great spy, except for the fact that she can't keep a secret."

"Yes, that would be a bit of a problem," said Ian with an amused look on his face, "although, I don't know that it's that she can't keep a secret as much as it is that she just doesn't want to. That would defeat the purpose of gaining all that information as far as she's concerned. She's a great girl though. Wally certainly thinks the world of her; I don't know where he'd be without her." Looking over Dervla's shoulder, he said, "And here she comes with your glasses of water and menus."

After Annie and Dervla had placed their orders, Ian said, "So, Andrew tells me that he came out to Grey Gables on Monday to see the inside of the house. That was quite a storm we had. We lost power over at Town Hall for at least an hour."

"So did we," said Annie, "but I was glad you came over anyway, Andrew. Did you tell Ian that you were out to Grey Gables this morning and asked Dervla to model for a painting?" asked Annie.

"Yes," said Andrew, "I had just mentioned it when you both came in." To Ian he said, "We'll be starting Saturday morning. Dervla is going to wear the wedding dress that Annie found in the attic."

"Wedding dress? I hadn't heard about that one. Is that

your newest mystery, Annie?" asked Ian.

"Sort of," said Annie. "I keep learning new things about it, but it seems that anyone who was connected with it has long since died. It has a link to Grey Gables, but it's more of a curiosity than a mystery, I guess."

"Considering the scrapes you've been in with some of your previous mysteries, I think something that's just a 'curiosity' might be welcomed!" said Ian. Then to Dervla he said, "That's quite an honor, Dervla, to be asked to be in one of Andrew's portraits. I've done some research on his work since Annie and I had lunch with him over at Maplehurst." Looking at Andrew he added, "Your paintings are amazing, Andrew, and that's just from seeing a few of them on a computer screen. I'm looking forward to seeing them in person."

Andrew smiled. "Thanks, Ian—I appreciate that, coming from you especially. I value your opinion." It seemed to Annie that Ian and Andrew had formed a friendship based on their mutual intellectual interests, and seeing that increased her respect for both men.

"I'm looking forward to seeing how it turns out," said Dervla. "I'm not familiar with Mr. Gareth's work, but Annie says he's the best, so it must be true!" They all laughed at that, but no one disputed her proposition.

There was a slight lull in the conversation as Peggy brought out their meals. After she left the table, Ian said, "So, ... Annie. ... Sounds like Dervla will be occupied most of the day on Saturday. I know a really nice restaurant down in Cape Elizabeth—it's less than two hours away—and I thought perhaps you and I could go there for lunch on Saturday. I could pick you up about ten thirty. It's a beautiful drive along the coastal area." Ian gave her a hopeful look, as he waited for her answer. Andrew and Dervla both smiled—Andrew watched Annie's face to see her reaction; Dervla looked at the table instead of looking at Annie, waiting to hear her reaction.

"I don't know, Ian ... Andrew and Dervla might need ... something," said Annie. "I'm not sure I should leave them ... alone."

Dervla looked up and said brightly, "Oh, we'll be fine, Annie. You should go and enjoy yourself. I don't want you to feel like you have to look after me all the time. And like Mr. Butler said, I'll be occupied with modeling for Mr. Gareth."

Annie looked doubtful.

Andrew spoke, "Yes, please go, Annie. The weather promises to be perfect on Saturday, so I'm hoping to work from fairly early in the morning and through the afternoon, to see which lighting is best for the effect I want to produce. I promise not to let any harm come to Dervla, or to your antique wedding dress."

Ian smiled at the encouragement the other two offered and then said to Annie, "I didn't want to bring this up, but you did promise that we would go for a meal sometime soon. I promise not to keep you out late. We'll have a nice leisurely lunch and then enjoy the sights in the area and easily be home before four o'clock in the afternoon."

Annie sighed. "It would be nice. ... OK. I'll be ready at ten thirty on Saturday morning."

"Great!" said Ian. "I'll be there on the dot."

~ 13 ~

Annie and Dervla spent the next couple of days working on their projects—Dervla made her petticoat, and Annie began her secret project for Dervla's hope-chest shower. Annie finally had a chance to go through her grandmother's crochet books and found a pattern that she thought would work nicely. It was a detachable collar made using Irish crochet techniques. The pattern called for crochet cotton thread and consisted of ten joined motifs with roses in the center of each one. It was delicate looking, and Annie thought it would look nice on Dervla, worn over a dark-color dress or sweater. Also, it met Annie's two other criteria—she was sure she could finish it in time, and it would be easy to hide from Dervla. Though Dervla wouldn't know the gift was for her, Annie didn't want her to see it beforehand—it was better for it to be a complete surprise.

For Dervla's project, Annie set up Gram's portable sewing machine on a small desk in what had been her mother's bedroom. The machine worked well, but it was old and only sewed a straight stitch. Annie wished she had thought to bring her sewing machine to Grey Gables from Texas—it was "new-fangled"—computerized with at least twenty stitch settings and the ability to make buttonholes almost automatically, it seemed. It was handy for a lot of things, but since she had been at Grey Gables, she had spent most of her craft time on crochet and hadn't needed a sewing machine for anything more than a few minor repairs.

Still, Gram's old one was a good machine for Dervla to use with her limited experience. It turned out that the petticoat pattern was fairly easy. After Dervla had cut out the pattern, she and Annie laid the fabric out on the kitchen table and cut out the pieces.

Annie explained a few seamstress techniques to Dervla, like staystitching, how to sew French seams so that the inside of the garment would be nice and neat, and how to grade the seams and under-stitch the facings to help them lay flat. There seemed to be no alternative but to do the buttonholes by hand, and though Annie hadn't worked any of those in ages, she hadn't forgotten the method and was able to show Dervla how to do it. Dervla practiced on scrap fabric until her buttonholes looked as good, or better, than machine-made buttonholes.

All in all, it was a good experience for both of them—for Dervla to learn, and for Annie to teach. And the petticoat turned out beautifully—it was feminine and well-made, and it was the perfect thing to wear under the wedding dress.

Annie went to pick up the dress on Friday. As Molly had promised, it was ready, and smelled fresh and clean. Molly had hung the dress on a padded hanger and placed it in a zippered, cotton garment bag. The wire had been reinserted into the wreath and the veil reattached; it looked even better than it had before. Along with the gloves, it had been placed in a cotton bag and boxed for storage. Just before Annie left, Molly handed her a CD in a slender case marked "Dawson Wedding Ensemble Photos." Annie thanked her and brought everything home to Grey Gables.

Andrew arrived Saturday morning just after the dew had burned away, and immediately began unloading his "studio" from his SUV and placing it out in the front yard. He was all business, setting up his easel and laying out the tools of his trade—his palette, tubes of oil paints, palette knives, brushes of all sizes, jars of linseed oil and turpentine, etc. Andrew had explained to Annie and Dervla that he wanted Dervla to stand, facing the ocean, in the front yard, so Annie gave him an old sheet to lay down on the ground to protect the dress from the grass. He spread that out on the ground where he wanted Dervla to stand.

While Andrew worked outside, Annie helped Dervla get into the wedding ensemble upstairs in her bedroom. Dervla put on the new petticoat she had made herself, with its pink ribbon and lace edging, while Annie once again began undoing the back buttons on the dress, stopping long enough to help Dervla with the buttons on the back of the slip. The day Dervla went shopping, she had purchased some opaque white pantyhose and white ballerina-type shoes with a small bow at the top of each. She put those on next. When the dress was unbuttoned, Annie lifted it over Dervla's head, and Dervla slipped her arms into the sleeves. Annie began the process of refastening the buttons. Dervla finished buttoning the cuffs and slipped on the crocheted gloves. Annie retrieved the veil and placed the wreath on Dervla's head, arranging the veil over the back of her hair and down her back.

She hadn't told Dervla about the prayer that Molly had found written in the stitches on the veil. She thought she would bring her laptop to the carriage house when they had the hope-chest shower, and she would show everyone the photographs that Molly had loaded on the disk, and tell them about Amanda Grey and the prayer she made for her daughter.

Annie stood back to look at Dervla in the wedding dress with the veil and gloves. She had thought that part of the effect she experienced when she first saw Dervla in the en-semble—the day of the storm—had been molded partially by the eeriness of the dark atmosphere and the flicker-ing candle flame. But as she looked at Dervla now, in the full light of a glorious summer morning, she had the same feeling she'd had then—Dervla seemed to glow. Whatever beauty Dervla possessed, both inner and outer, was magni-fied by the wedding dress ensemble in a way that Annie was at a loss to explain.

Dervla was ready to go outside to stand for the portrait. With her two gloved hands, she lifted the front of the dress well off the floor so that the lower part of her legs and her feet, all clad in white, were exposed; Annie picked up the train, and together they made their way down the staircase, out onto the porch and into the yard.

Andrew looked up and smiled. He didn't appear to be shocked as he had the first time he'd seen Dervla, but he actually seemed rather amused. Annie supposed the sight of two women trying so hard to protect the dress from any contact with the carpet of grass struck him funny somehow. *Men*, she thought.

Once Dervla was standing safely on the sheet, Andrew came over to place her as he wanted for the painting. Annie watched for a while. First, Andrew placed his hands on Dervla's shoulders to turn her slightly; then he moved the positions of both her hands. Next he touched her chin to tilt her head just so. Then he walked back to his position by his easel to look at her, his eyes taking in every detail. Again he walked over to Dervla to move the train of the dress; he lifted the bottom of the veil, and then he picked up and twisted the wreath slightly and placed it back on her head. He walked back over to the easel to look at her again. He continued this back and forth—positioning and then observing—again and again. There were the things he couldn't change, but took into account at any rate. Andrew looked at the position of the sun, the shadow cast by a tree, the effect of the wind on Dervla's hair. ... The whole process was absolutely painstaking. And he hadn't even started painting yet.

Annie decided she had better go and change for her date with Ian. Yes. There, she'd said it. It was a date. It was a date with a friend, it was true, but it seemed silly not to call it what it was. It was a lunch date, but knowing Ian she expected it was a very nice restaurant, so she thought she should dress up more than she would for a bite at The Cup & Saucer. Annie opted for a sleeveless dress with a black bodice and a black-and-white geometric print skirt that was fitted down to the top of the hips and then flared out in several pleats down to the hem. With big sunglasses propped on top of her head, and black flats on her feet, she felt very Audrey Hepburn-like.

As promised, Ian arrived precisely at ten thirty. Annie invited him in while she finished transferring the contents of her everyday purse to one that was more compact and more in keeping with her outfit.

"You look super," said Ian. He had dressed up a bit more than usual for a Saturday noon lunch too, and looked very handsome in a sport jacket with a button-down shirt open at the neck and light-color slacks.

"So do you," said Annie, smiling. "Just let me tuck one more thing in my purse, and I'll be ready to go."

"That's quite a production going on out there. Is that the wedding dress you found in the attic then?" asked Ian.

"It is. I don't know if you got a good look at Dervla in the dress, but she's absolutely stunning in it. I hope we'll get to see the painting when we come back. I'm not sure if this is just a preliminary thing, or the actual painting. You should've seen Andrew arranging everything just so. He's a stickler for detail."

Annie stooped over and picked up a small cooler she'd placed by the front door. "Could I get you to carry this out, Ian?"

Ian got a puzzled look on his face. "Uh … the invitation was for me to take you out to a nice restaurant for lunch … are you expecting to be extra hungry?"

Annie laughed. "It's not for us! I meant for you to carry it out and place under that tree nearest Andrew and Dervla. You should have seen us trying to get her across the lawn without dragging the dress through it. I thought they might just stay outside for lunch. I put some water and sandwiches with a bag of ice in the cooler. I'm going to carry out a couple of folding stools from Gramps's old camping set, and a bag with cups and napkins."

"You seem to have thought of everything," said Ian. "You like looking out for other people, don't you?"

"Can't deny it," replied Annie simply. "I'm ready to go when you are."

*   *   *   *

As promised, Ian returned Annie to Grey Gables before four o'clock in the afternoon. The meal at the restaurant had been wonderful, and the location provided a magnificent view of the ocean from their table. Then they'd visited the lighthouse and museum located in the same vicinity, and Ian even drove her past a castle that was purported to be haunted.

When they pulled into the drive, they saw that Dervla was still standing on the sheet in the yard, though Andrew was in the process of moving her to a slightly different position than Annie had seen her in that morning. He was using the same back-and-forth technique that Annie had observed earlier.

Dervla looked different. Her hair was arranged in an upswept style on top of her head; she was no longer wearing the veil and gloves, and there was no sign of them. Annie thought that Dervla or Andrew must have taken them inside. She hoped the items were upstairs in Dervla's room and the door was closed. She hated to think what Boots would do to the pieces given the opportunity.

"I hope those two took a break," said Ian.

"I'm sure they did," said Annie. "See—the camp stools have been used. I might make some fresh lemonade to drink. Would you care for any? We can take it out to share with them."

"That would be very nice, thank you."

They made their way inside, apparently unnoticed by the artist and his model. Annie checked the living room; no veil or gloves, and Boots was contentedly stretched out on the sofa. Annie heaved a sigh of relief. She and Ian headed on back to the kitchen.

As Annie was reaching into the cabinet for drinking glasses, she said, "I'm not used to being taken out for Saturday lunch—I had such a good time. Thanks for inviting me, Ian."

"Not at—" Ian began, but stopped suddenly at the muffled sound of men shouting outside. He and Annie looked at each other with puzzled expressions for a moment. "What is tha—" he began to say when he was cut off again by a woman's scream. Annie dropped the glass she was holding when she heard the scream and it crashed to the floor, breaking into pieces. Ian ran into the hall and through the front door; Annie was right on his heels.

As she got to the edge of the porch she could see what the commotion was. In the yard, violently wrestling in the grass, were Andrew Gareth and Tony Palmer. Dervla was crying hysterically and trying to get them to stop, but she didn't dare get in the middle of the struggling men. Tony seemed to have the upper hand—he was younger and fitter. Ian got to them as quickly as he could and didn't hesitate to try to pull Tony and Andrew apart. Ian was shouting for them to stop, and was nearly knocked off his feet more than once, but at last he succeeded.

Tony sat to Ian's left, wiping blood that was running from his nose with the back of his hand; even so, his expression was still belligerent, as if he was considering going after the older man again. Ian gave him his handkerchief and told him in no uncertain terms to sit tight.

Andrew appeared to be the worse off of the two. Breathing heavily, he lay on his back in the grass moaning slightly. Annie knelt down and leaned over him to assess the damage. The area next to his left eye was red, and would surely be black and blue in short order; his lower lip had split and was bleeding slightly, but at least his eyes seemed clear and alert. Annie didn't doubt that he was bruised all over and would feel every bit of it for days to come.

Dervla was in shock. She had fallen to her knees, and her face was streaked with tears as she looked at the two men, first Tony, and then Andrew, and then back again. Annie wanted to comfort her, but she thought the primary thing was to tend to the wounds of Andrew and Tony. She checked the cooler, but the ice she had put in it that morning had melted.

To Ian, Annie said, "I'll be right back—I'm going to get some ice from the freezer."

As she ran back toward the house, she heard Ian begin to address the two men, "What in the blazes …"

In the kitchen, minding the broken glass, Annie looked in the freezer and realized she had no ice cubes. She remembered now that she had been in a hurry that morning when she emptied the trays and had meant to refill them when she got home. She rummaged around for something she could use instead. She had a bag of frozen cauliflower

and a bag of frozen broccoli. Those were going to have to
do. She grabbed the vegetables and a couple of dish towels,
and ran back outside.

Tony was gone. She looked around and saw him walking
up the street toward Wedgwood. Andrew was sitting up now,
and when Annie got to him, she wrapped a towel around
one of the packages of vegetables and handed it to him. He
thanked her and held the package against the left side of his
face, over his eye, wincing as he did so.

"Annie," Ian said quietly, "why don't you take Dervla
upstairs and help her change. I'm going to run Andrew over
to see Doc Witham to make sure he's all right."

Annie nodded and looked into Ian's eyes, saying "thank
you" without speaking a word. She helped Dervla to her
feet, and steadied her as they walked back toward the house.
Annie picked up the hem of the wedding dress, but she was
more concerned about keeping Dervla from tripping on it
than she was about the dress. Inside Grey Gables, as she
and Dervla climbed the staircase, Annie heard car doors
slam and the sound of Ian's car as he started it and pulled
out of the drive.

Dervla still had not said a word. Annie wanted to ask
her what had happened, but it seemed better to help get
her out of the wedding dress first, and perhaps fix her a cup
of tea. Then she could try to get to the bottom of what had
caused the fight.

As Annie helped Dervla out of the dress, she saw the
veil and gloves lying on the bed. It was as she had hoped—
one of them had brought the veil and gloves upstairs and
had had the foresight to close the door. Annie put them

away in the box Molly had provided and placed it on a shelf in the closet.

When Annie had finished putting away the dress, she offered Dervla some tea and something to eat, but she refused, saying she just wanted to lie down for a while. Her eyes still brimmed with tears, and Annie thought it was best to let her cry if she needed to. There would be enough time for talking later.

Annie changed her clothes into something more suitable for a late Saturday afternoon at home and cleaned up the broken glass in the kitchen. A short time later, Ian called her on his cell phone from the hospital to let her know that Andrew was going to be all right. Doc Witham, who had been a trusted family doctor in Stony Point for almost forty years, had insisted that Andrew go to the emergency room for X-rays; fortunately, there were no broken bones and no sign of a concussion. It was lucky for Andrew—and for Tony.

Ian told Annie what happened while she went to fetch the ice. He said that first he had asked Tony what had gotten into him. Ian admitted, "I may not have said that in the friendliest of terms." Tony was apparently still angry over something, Ian didn't know what, and just said, "None of your business," and then got up and walked away.

Ian then asked Andrew if he felt well enough to sit up and wanted to ask him how the fight had started, but upon seeing Andrew's condition, he thought it was better to save it for later. It was only after Andrew was given the all-clear by the doctor that Ian asked Andrew any questions.

"According to Andrew," said Ian, "he was standing in front of Dervla, positioning her for the portrait, turning her face for better lighting of her profile when Tony just attacked him out of nowhere. I had to ask him if he wanted to press charges and offered to call Chief Edwards, but Andrew said no. Like I said, it was lucky for Tony that Andrew wasn't more seriously hurt."

"I don't understand why Tony was even at Grey Gables," Annie said. "He wasn't supposed to be back from Boston until Monday." She paused and then said, "I watched Andrew work with Dervla before I went up to change for our … date. I think I understand how someone might look at that situation from a distance and think it was more intimate than it actually was."

"I never thought of Tony Palmer as a hothead, but even so, his behavior was so far out of line. Even I could see how distraught Dervla was, but Tony never acknowledged her before he left to see if she was all right. I'd never treat the woman I loved in such a manner," Ian said.

Annie smiled, and was glad they were talking over the phone and not face to face. "Dervla is still up in her room. I can't persuade her to come downstairs, and she said she doesn't want me to bring anything up to her. I'm worried."

"Just give her some time," said Ian. "I'm sure that things will look better in the morning."

"I hope so," said Annie.

"Andrew asked me to bring him back to Grey Gables when he's finished here so he can collect his gear and get his car, though I'm not sure he should be driving. How would you feel about driving him back downtown? Then I could drive you home."

"I'd rather not leave Dervla alone," said Annie, "but I

guess it won't take too long. I'll just have to let her know that I'll be gone for a little while."

∼ 14 ∼

nnie was watching out the window for Ian to return with Andrew when she saw Alice's flashy red convertible pull into the drive at the carriage house. Annie went outside and walked the short distance across the lawn to Alice's home. Alice saw her and waved, and then leaned against the car waiting to talk to her.

"Where have you been all day?" asked Annie.

"District meeting in Portland for Divine Décor," Alice answered, yawning. "I had to leave at dark o'clock this morning to get there for the eight o'clock meeting. I'm not used to early hours. I'm beat. What's been going on here today?"

"It's a long story, which I intend to tell you in full, but Ian and Andrew are going to be here shortly, and I have to drive Andrew to Maplehurst Inn."

At that comment, Alice's eyebrows raised and her mouth opened as if she was about to ask a question. Annie saw the look and raised her hand, "No questions yet. But I have a favor to ask. I know you're tired, but would you come over and stay with Dervla? She's upstairs in her room, and she's upset, and I don't really want to leave her alone. I don't think she'll be coming out, but if she does, I want her to know that someone is there."

Alice looked at Annie expression and simply said, "Of course. Just let me change, and I'll be right over."

Annie gave Alice a quick hug and said, "You're the best. Thanks, Alice. I'll see you at the house."

Alice appeared at Annie's door ten minutes later, dressed in a yellow T-shirt that had "I ♥ Maine" written in blue letters across the front, cotton pajama bottoms, and flip-flops. She carried her project bag with her, saying, "If Dervla's upstairs, I'm going to try to get some work done on her present for the shower. I can stash it away if I hear her coming down the steps."

"Thanks again for coming over. There isn't time for all the details right now; I'm not even sure what exactly happened myself, but just so you know the basics—Andrew and Tony had a fight in my front yard this afternoon. Ian took Andrew to the hospital for X-rays. He's all right, but we're a little worried about him driving, so I'm going to drive Andrew's car back to Maplehurst, and then Ian will bring me home."

"That's really all you're going to tell me?" asked Alice.

Annie heard the sound of Ian's car pulling into the driveway. "Yep—but only for the time being. I will definitely fill you in when I get home. I may understand this all better by then myself. Help yourself to something to eat and drink. You know where everything is." And with that Annie stepped outside.

The sun was low in the sky, its angle casting long shadows, and Annie imagined that they made the familiar scene look very surreal after the violence she had witnessed there earlier. She wanted to scrub that image from her mind, but it was hard to forget. What should have been a fine summer evening was tainted with the aftereffects of the fight.

Andrew and Ian had just gotten out of the car. Andrew was walking slowly, as if every move was painful. The red splotch she had seen on his face earlier had turned into a real shiner that encircled his left eye. It looked like he had a couple of stitches in his bottom lip.

"Andrew, what can I do to help you?" said Annie.

"I'll need to straighten up my work area and put away my supplies. When that's done, I'd appreciate help getting the car loaded up. There are a couple of canvases, and they'll still be wet, so we'll have to be careful with those—I'll lay them in the back of the car myself if you don't mind. You may want to collect your sheet and the cooler. Thanks so much for thinking of all those things, by the way. It was really helpful—especially the camp stools—it gave Dervla a chance to rest now and then." He paused for a moment. "Is she all right?"

"I think she's still in shock. She's been in her room ever since you left, and won't come out. I've offered to take her something to eat or drink, but she's refusing everything. Maybe a good night's sleep will make a difference." Annie wanted to ask Andrew more questions, but she thought it wasn't the right time, so she set to work, picking up the sheet to shake off the grass.

Ian grabbed the cooler and stools and said, "I'll just run these up to the house."

"Alice is inside," said Annie. "She's going to stay at Grey Gables while we take Andrew home, just so that Dervla won't be alone."

Ian just smiled and said, "Good idea."

Annie gave the sheet a couple of shakes and started to

fold it up. She took a step back and nearly fell when she stepped on a small object that threw her off balance. She leaned over to look and found a small, green velvet–covered jewelry box. Curious, she opened it to see a gorgeous engagement ring. In the center was a sparkling clear diamond and around it, small petal-shaped green emeralds. She took it out of the box to look inside to see if the ring had been engraved—it had. It said simply, "Mavourneen"—the Irish Gaelic word Dervla had said meant "my beloved," and the name of the place where she and Tony had met. Annie put the ring back in the box.

She walked over to show Andrew. He was intent on putting his supplies away and didn't realize she was standing beside him. She didn't say anything at first, but just held the opened box in front of him and watched his expression as it came into his field of vision. He was puzzled. "Beautiful ring. Where did it come from?" he asked.

"I found it in the grass just now. It must have fallen out of Tony's pocket during the fight," said Annie.

"You think he was coming over to formally propose to Dervla when he attacked me?" asked Andrew.

"I'm not sure what was in his head. The fact that he had it with him indicates that must have been his plan. I wish I could understand what happened," said Annie.

"Well, if you figure it out, please tell me," said Andrew. "I was just working, moving Dervla to a different position—I heard him shout something, and then he was there in my face. I don't even know what he said really. He knocked me back and started swinging. It was like he was crazed. He was so angry."

Ian walked out of the house and joined them. Annie showed him the ring. He raised his eyebrows and said, "The plot thickens."

*　　*　　*　　*

After all of Andrew's supplies and canvases were loaded in his SUV, Annie drove him downtown. He insisted that he needed to unload his supplies, or the paintings at the very least. She parked in front of Dress to Impress since Andrew had rented space above the clothing store to use as his studio.

Andrew got out and unlocked a side door that was next to the store's front. Behind the door was a small vestibule. Across from the door to the right there was a freight elevator; to the left of that there was a flight of stairs that bordered a brick-sided wall. Andrew grabbed one of the paintings from the back of the SUV and headed inside and up the steps. Annie thought he seemed to be moving a lot slower than he usually did.

Ian had parked behind them, and from Andrew's car he picked up the small folding table and easel to carry up, while Annie grabbed the vinyl-sided bag and another carrying case that Andrew used for supplies. They followed him up the stairs, matching their pace to his. When they reached the top, there was a landing with another door that Andrew unlocked.

Inside, Annie saw it was one large open room with long blind-covered windows at the front and back. Andrew flipped a switch and the entire room was bathed in light.

It was just what she expected an artist's studio to look

like. There were various easels and painted canvases sitting around, and there were several long tables—one was covered with sketches and photographs, another had stacks of books and writing materials—for research, she supposed. There were shelves full of books and other shelves full of art supplies. It looked chaotic, but not in an unpleasant way. It was like a great creative spirit had been let loose. Annie thought it was wonderful.

Andrew placed the painting he had carried up on a ledge along the side of the room. "I'll get the other one in just a minute," he said, leaning against a table for a moment.

"Please let me get it, Andrew," said Ian. "I promise I'll be careful."

"OK," said Andrew. "I must be getting old—I feel absolutely done in."

"That's what happens when an older man gets involved in a brawl," teased Ian. "I'll be right back up."

While Ian went to get the second painting, Annie looked at the painting Andrew had just set on the ledge. With all the excitement of the afternoon, Annie hadn't looked at the canvases to see what he had done that day.

This painting showed Dervla as Annie had seen her that morning: She looked toward the ocean to the right, her face in profile with the sun lighting up her complexion in pinks and peaches. Her long, dark hair, with highlights of red, hung down over her shoulders, and the veil seemed to billow out slightly in the wind. She held a single pink rose in her gloved hand as it rested on the side of the dress's skirt. Grey Gables sat in the background to the left, looking its best, like it was brand-new and had never been in disrepair.

Somehow, Andrew had captured the dress, gloves, and veil, not photographically, but in such a way that the mind filled in details easily. Annie could almost swear that she could count the stitches on the crochet. There were multiple layers of different shades of green in the grass and the leaves on the trees, and the sliver of ocean was deep blue with peaks of white on the choppy waves. The painting conveyed movement and vivacity.

Ian returned with the second painting and set it next to the first one on the ledge. While he went to look at the other paintings in the room, Annie turned her attention to that one. She almost gasped at the contrast she saw there. It was more than the absence of the veil and gloves, and the change in Dervla's hairstyle. The model faced the artist this time. Annie said to herself "model" instead of "Dervla" because she no longer felt that it was Dervla, but some other person's face that looked out at her. This woman's hair and eyes were darker than Dervla's, but somehow the face was familiar, as if she'd seen her before. The expression on her face was solemn, but not sad.

The wedding dress was different too. Whereas the crocheted trim on the dress was clearly visible on the first painting, it was completely absent from this one. The high collar stood bare with no embellishment on it or below it, and the cuffs were the same plain fabric as the dress. The woman clasped her hands together in front, close to her body, her fingers interlaced; Annie wasn't sure if it was an anxious or pleading gesture, or if it indicated a posture of prayer. It seemed to be somewhere in between.

Grey Gables took on a different face too. Instead of

benignly sitting off to one side, Andrew had painted it directly behind the woman so that it seemed to loom over
her menacingly. Gone were the cheerful colors of the first
painting. All the tones of this painting were gray, as if a fine
film of silver dust overlayed the scene. Instead of motion
and life, it was like a moment caught in time where change
could never happen.

Annie shivered involuntarily. Ian was on the other side
of the room, but Andrew was watching Annie.

"Slightly different in feel, wouldn't you say?" he asked.

Annie looked at him, but couldn't seem to find words
to speak.

"I was going to show this to you later, but I think now
might be the time."

With that, he walked to the table where Annie had laid
his vinyl-sided bag and reached inside. On the day of the
storm, in the library, he had removed his drawing pad and
pencils from the same bag, but this time, he removed an
old leather-covered folder. When he opened it and handed
it to her, Annie could see that it wasn't just a folder, but
a double-sided picture frame. Within each frame was an
antique black-and-white photograph.

She studied each picture with intense interest. In the
left-hand photograph there was a round-cheeked baby with
a cherub's mouth, the picture of health, propped up against
a pillow and dressed in a long, gleaming white christening
gown. The baby's lace-trimmed bonnet had been carefully
placed on the blanket next to it, and the gown was arranged
to show its finery. The baby had a swirl of black hair on its
head and curious dark eyes that stared at something beside

the camera; its delicate fingers were curled into two tiny
fists.

In the facing frame was a photograph of a couple on
their wedding day. The man was obviously older than his
bride, his neatly trimmed beard streaked with white. He sat
in a straight-back, wooden chair; his own back was equally straight. The chair was slightly turned so that his body
faced toward the left of the photograph. He was dressed in
a captain's uniform—a double-breasted jacket with metal
buttons and the insignia of his rank on the sleeves, over a
starched white shirt with a stand-up collar; around his neck
he had tied a dark cravat. His captain's hat was perched
upon his knee, and his highly polished black shoes glinted
in the photographer's lights.

The man looked at the camera with steady eyes and
an unsmiling mouth. People usually didn't smile for photographs in those days; part of that had to do with the amount
of time the camera's lens had to be left open for an expo-
sure. Nevertheless, Annie had the impression that it was not
his habit to smile much on any occasion. His skin appeared
to be slightly weathered from contact with the sun and wind
on the sea, but there were no prominent laugh lines in the
outer corners of his eyes. While his countenance was not
forbidding, it was, at least, stern, and she had the sense
that he would not be a man who was easily swayed, either
by circumstance or emotion.

The bride was standing to the left of her new husband,
and slightly behind him, to show the full length of her white
wedding gown. Her hair and eyes appeared to be the same
dark color as the child's in the other photograph. Her hair

was arranged on top of her head, and a veil that looked like it was made of organdy covered her from the top of her head, over her shoulders, and down her back to her knees. In her hands, she held a massive bouquet of formally arranged white roses. Her expression was serious, but there was a hint of a smile at the corners of her mouth, and her eyes gazed at the camera as if looking into the future, full of confidence and hope.

Annie was unconsciously holding her breath. She looked up from the woman in the photograph to the woman in the second painting. Not only was it the same face, it was the same wedding dress. The very same dress Annie had found in the attic. She was sure of it. It had the same high collar, the puffy sleeves with long cuffs, the fitted waist, the lower ruffle around the hem. But, like the second painting, there was no crochet—not around the neck, nor on the cuffs. The bride wasn't wearing gloves, and the veil was completely different.

Annie looked up at Andrew. He was watching her reaction as she was studying the photographs. Annie asked him, "Is this Amanda and Captain Grey?"

"Yes, it is," he answered.

"And is this the same wedding dress that I found in the attic?" she asked.

"I believe so."

Ian had come to stand next to Annie, and she handed the photographs to him so he could see them as well, while Annie tried to make sense of all the information with which she was being bombarded.

"Who is the baby in the photograph?" asked Annie.

"That is Lydia Grey, the only child of Amanda and Zacharias; she was born in 1898," replied Andrew.

"How ... I mean, where did you find these pictures?" Annie asked Andrew.

He paused for moment, seeming to consider if he wanted to reveal his sources.

"I didn't find them actually. I borrowed them ... from my oldest sister," he answered. "They were given to her by our father, who had received them from his mother before she died at the age of 92."

"And how did your father's mother come to have the photographs?" asked Annie.

"They were a gift from her parents. My grandmother's maiden name was Lydia Grey; Amanda and Zacharias Grey were my great-grandparents."

— 15 —

nnie was shocked into silence for a moment, and Ian seemed to be the same. Annie's mind began to race with things she wanted to ask Andrew, but then she noticed that he had grabbed hold of the edge of the table to steady himself. She'd been so enrapt looking at the paintings and the photographs that she'd forgotten that he was injured.

"I have a million questions, Andrew, but we need to get you to Maplehurst so you can rest now." She looked at Ian and could tell that he was concerned too. The three of them went back down the stairs, Ian first, in case Andrew started to falter. When they got to the inn, Annie dropped Andrew off at the front entrance and went to park his car in the inn's parking lot while Ian parked out front and went inside with Andrew to make sure he made it to his room. Annie waited by Ian's car until he came back out to let her in.

"Do you think it's all right for him to be here alone?" asked Annie. "Maybe he should have stayed at Grey Gables."

"I think he's all right, Annie," answered Ian. "I think he's just exhausted. The doctor gave him the all clear. A good night's sleep is what we all need, I think. What a day! Let's get you home."

After Ian saw Annie to the door at Grey Gables, she walked in to find the house dark and quiet. In the living room she looked over the edge of the sofa to find Alice sound asleep. She was lying on her back, covered with an afghan and Boots was curled up on her tummy. It seemed unnecessary to wake her, so Annie wrote a note and left it where Alice was bound to see it if she woke up—on top of her project bag—and went upstairs to get ready for bed herself. She'd forgotten to eat any dinner, but she was too tired to worry about it.

Her dreams that night were full of the events from the day—helping Dervla into the wedding dress, the drive along the coast with Ian, the fight in the front yard, seeing Andrew's battered face, and watching Tony walk away from Grey Gables ... these were interwoven with the images from Andrew's paintings, and the faces of the people in the photographs he had shown her. She heard a woman's voice saying the words, "Dear Father in Heaven, please hear my prayer ..."

She woke with a start, and the sun was streaming through the window. Boots had jumped on the bed and was standing on her chest, her face nuzzling Annie's chin. Part of Annie felt like scolding the chubby cat, but instead she scratched Boots's ears and talked to her in a soothing voice, assuring her that breakfast would be forthcoming as soon as Annie could pull herself out of bed.

Out in the hallway, the house still sounded quiet, so Annie tiptoed to the stairs, but stepped on the same floorboard that always creaked at the top of the stairs, and which everyone who went up and down the stairs seemed to hit without fail. Once she made it to the bottom of the stairs she tiptoed into the living room and was just about to peek over the sofa to see if Alice was still there.

"Good morning, sleepyhead!"

Annie jumped and turned around to see Alice standing in the hallway, smiling, holding a glass of orange juice in her hand.

"Alice! You scared the bejeebers out of me! What are you doing sneaking around this time of the morning?" asked Annie.

"Ummm … I wasn't sneaking … I heard the upstairs floorboard creak and came out of the kitchen to find you tiptoeing into the living room. That looked pretty sneaky to me."

"I was trying to be considerate," said Annie.

"How? By hovering over me like my mother, and then saying 'Get up, Alice! Daylight's a burnin'!'?" asked Alice with a laugh.

Annie considered the idea. "No, that's not my style. I prefer a good-morning song. I used to wake LeeAnn with it. She loved it when she was little, but it drove her crazy when she was a teenager. I must say it provided me with much amusement during those latter years," she said with a grin.

"Well, I am sorry that I missed that. Maybe next time," said Alice.

"Has there been any sign of Dervla this morning?" asked Annie.

"Not yet. Why don't we make some coffee, and you can fill me in about what happened yesterday. Honestly, if I hadn't been so tired, I might never have gotten to sleep after hearing your sketchy outline of the day's events. It was hard to concentrate on my cross-stitch, so I just put it away and lay down on the sofa under one of your afghans, and Boots joined me. The next thing I knew it was daylight. Found your note, by the way. Thanks for letting me know you were home."

"It was the least I could do. Thanks for being here. You really are the best," said Annie. "Let's go make that coffee." She felt Boots winding between her ankles. "And feed Boots," she added.

Alice wanted to know every detail; Annie started with Saturday morning and told her everything up to the point where she came home that evening, including the revelation that Andrew Gareth was the great-grandson of the very same Captain Grey who had built Grey Gables.

"What did you do with the engagement ring you found?" asked Alice.

"Oh, I put it in the library on the shelf," Annie said.

"What are you going to do with it?"

"The only thing I can do really—I'll walk over to Wedgwood this afternoon and give it to Tony, unless he comes over here first. I don't want Dervla to see it, or to know about it until he shows it to her, when he's down on one knee, asking her to marry him."

"Do you think that's still going to happen?" asked Alice.

"I don't know. I really don't understand what happened yesterday. It was like Tony was primed for a confrontation," said Annie.

"It might have been Gwen's doing, you know. She said that she and John were trying to talk Tony out of the marriage."

"I just can't imagine what she could have told him that would elicit so much anger—especially since it was directed at Andrew." Annie sighed and said, "I dread going over there. I hope Tony's settled down. More than that, I hope he'll come here to apologize to Dervla."

Just then, they both heard the telltale creak of the upstairs floorboard. Annie went out into the hall just as Dervla was about halfway down the steps. Trying to sound somewhat cheery, she said, "Good morning, Dervla! I hope you slept well." One look at her face told the story; Annie doubted that Dervla had slept at all. "Come and join us in the kitchen. Alice is here, and we have coffee, and I'm sure we can rustle up something to go with it."

"Thanks, Annie. That would be nice."

Dervla sat down at the kitchen table with a big mug of coffee while Annie and Alice fussed about making breakfast and ended up deciding that pancakes were called for. Alice was the expert, so she worked on that while Annie fried some bacon and warmed the syrup. It was American-style comfort food—Annie hoped it agreed with Dervla's Irish palate.

Dervla did eat a little, but Annie thought it might have been more to be polite than out of any real appetite. When they had finished eating, Dervla said, "I have a favor to ask, Annie. I was wondering if you could take me up to Boothbay Harbor for mass this morning. I think it's the closest Catholic Church—at least that's where Tony took me last week." At the mention of his name, her eyes looked wet with tears, but none fell.

"Of course," said Annie. "I've heard that the church there is one of the prettiest around. If you don't mind, I'll join you for the service. I've only been in a Catholic Church once before, and that was for a friend's wedding."

"If it's all right," said Alice, "I'll join you too. I just need to run home to shower and change. How soon do we need to leave?"

Dervla had the bulletin from the previous week and checked the time for the service. Figuring in the time they needed to get there, they decided to leave the dishes in the sink and start getting ready right away.

Thirty minutes later, in what they were certain was some sort of record, they were in Annie's Malibu and headed down the road. Looking at the map, Alice, the navigator, said they could've gotten there faster by boat, but since they didn't have one, she thought they would make it just in time. Annie and Alice tried to keep a light conversation going, avoiding anything to do with Tony or wedding dresses. Dervla sat in the backseat and seemed to be listening, but said very little.

They did make it just in time, and sat near the back. It was a beautiful chapel, located near the water. Many parts of the service were different from what Annie was used to, but the creed was similar, and she recognized a couple of the hymns that they sang. The readings from the Bible always spoke to her at her home church, and it was no different here. The priest's homily was short and to the point; she preferred Reverend Wallace's sermons, but she still appreciated the message. She joined in the prayers for those in need, and when the priest said, "Peace be with you," she joined in with the congregational reply, "and also with you." She and Alice stayed in their seats when Dervla went up front for Holy Communion, but other than that Annie found that she could worship there as well as anywhere. Annie remembered as a teenager that Gram had told her—the purpose of church is to worship and honor God, not just to visit with your friends. Annie was glad to blend her voice with others for that purpose, even if they had a few different ideas than she did. She was sure that was true even in her own church.

On the way home, Dervla's spirits seemed improved, and she joined in the conversation more readily than she had earlier. When they were almost back to Grey Gables, she said, "Thanks for taking me to church today. And thank you for your friendship. It's been wonderful to be here and to get to know you." She paused for a moment before continuing. "I ... I've made a decision. I thought about it all night, but going to church today helped me to be at peace with it. I'm going to go back to Ireland. It's my home, ... and I think that Tony has changed his mind about me."

She stopped talking as her voice started to break a bit.

"What about you?" asked Annie. "Have you changed your mind about him?"

Dervla didn't speak for a moment, and Annie could see in the rearview mirror that she was holding back tears. "No," she said quietly, "I haven't changed my mind. Remember when we talked last week about my mother, and how she made sure I memorized poetry?"

"Yes," Annie said, "I remember. We said it was like a gift, that the words would come to us when we needed wisdom."

"Well, there's a sonnet by Shakespeare that goes in part like this:

'Let me not to the marriage of true minds

Admit impediments. Love is not love
Which alters when it alteration finds,
Or bends with the remover to remove:
O, no! it is an ever-fixed mark
That looks on tempests and is never shaken.'"

"That's beautiful, Dervla," said Alice. "I've never heard that before."

"Well, that's how I feel about Tony. I love him, and nothing will change that. I'm not saying that it's not ever going to work out, but … I think he needs time, and his family … at least part of his family … needs time. His parents may never accept me, but my being here is no good if it drives him to behave as he did yesterday. He's too good to be like that. I know him. And I don't want to be the cause of turning him into a jealous, angry man. It would break my heart to see that, and I won't do it."

*   *   *   *

By late in the afternoon, there had been no sign of Tony. Dervla was on Annie's laptop, using the Internet to look for an economical flight back to Ireland, so Annie decided it was time to take the engagement ring to Wedgwood and give it back to Tony. Only saying to Dervla that she was going out for a walk, Annie put the small box in her pocket and set out, walking up Ocean Drive to the Palmers' house.

She wasn't sure if she should go to the back door she had entered the last time she was at Wedgwood, when Tony and Dervla had first arrived, or go to the front. She decided the front door was more appropriate on this occasion.

She walked up the concrete walkway, edged on either side with rows of red-orange–flowering nasturtiums, to the front door. She rang the bell and waited a few moments; Gwen appeared at the door. Annie hadn't seen her since the last Hook and Needle Club meeting. She knew that Mary Beth had talked to Gwen and told her that they were going ahead with the shower—*the shower!*—Annie had completely forgotten about that. What were they going to do now? She'd have to call the other members of the club when she got home, or maybe she could wait until the meeting on Tuesday; it couldn't make much difference now—she was sure the others would have already started on their projects too.

Gwen's manner was strange—not friendly, but not unfriendly either. Annie wasn't sure how to read her, so she just tried to keep a normal tone. "Hi, Gwen. Is Tony at home? I have something I need to return to him."

Gwen looked slightly uncomfortable. "He's not here. He left yesterday. I don't know where he is."

"He left? Without even saying goodbye to Dervla or apologizing?" asked Annie, her voice rising in tone as she spoke.

Gwen looked embarrassed. "Please come in, Annie. I think we need to talk. I don't really know what happened, but whatever it was it … it may have been my fault."

Annie went into the front room, and she and Gwen sat facing each other on the sofa. It appeared that Gwen was alone. "John went to play golf this afternoon. He won't be home for a little while yet. Please tell me what happened at Grey Gables yesterday. Tony was angry when he left here, and he came back a very short time afterward. He didn't even come in the house to say goodbye—he just got in his car and left. I had looked out the window just in time to see him as he backed the car out of the driveway."

Annie explained, as much as she knew, the events that transpired on Saturday afternoon. When she told Gwen how Andrew had been injured, and that Ian had taken him to the hospital, she was horrified.

"Oh, Annie! What have I done?" said Gwen.

Annie was puzzled about how it could have been Gwen's fault; she asked her quietly, "What did you do, Gwen?"

"I know it was wrong, but I was trying to put Dervla in a … let's say, a less favorable light. I told myself that I was doing it for Tony's own good." She paused, looking into Annie's face to see if she understood, but Annie couldn't find it in her to approve of Gwen's reasoning.

Gwen continued, "I saw her, Dervla, with that man who's been to your house—Tony told me he was an artist—out in the yard, and they looked rather chummy, I thought, and then Peggy told me that she'd seen you and Dervla sitting with Ian and the artist at The Cup & Saucer." She paused again and looked down at her hands. "Tony came home early from Boston on Saturday. He's accepted a really good job there, and was excited about it and was going to walk over to Grey Gables to tell Dervla. He showed me an engagement ring he bought for her, and said there was no reason to delay the wedding now. I was desperate to stop him. I … I told Tony that Dervla had been seen out differ-ent places with that man while he was gone. I may have … exaggerated a little bit … and I didn't mention that you and

Ian were with them at The Cup & Saucer."

"Gwen! How could you do such a thing?" Annie was truly shocked.

Gwen started to cry. "I don't know why I did it. He's my youngest—my boy—I just couldn't bear to see him married to a girl like that."

"A girl like what, Gwen?" said Annie, starting to get angry herself.

"Tony told me—he met her in a pub—where she was performing with some sort of band. Her parents were 'artists.' I doubt they ever did a day's work in their lives. She was orphaned young. She couldn't have had a very good upbringing."

Now Annie was livid. "You don't know her at all! You've made no effort to know her! You decided as soon as she walked in your door that she wasn't good enough for your son. Let me tell you something, Gwen. I *have* gotten to know Dervla, and I think that it may be the case that she is entirely *too* good for your son. She's at Grey Gables right now making a plane reservation to fly home to Ireland. She loves your son so much that she'd rather go than cause him or his family pain, even though it's breaking her heart. Every assumption you've made about her and her 'upbringing' is dead wrong."

Gwen was stunned into silence. Annie had never talked to her that way before; in fact, no one had ever talked to her that way before.

Annie calmed down a little since she'd had her say. "Tony dropped the engagement ring in the yard during the fight. That's why I came here today—to bring it back to him. I didn't tell Dervla that I had it. Would you please see that he gets it? I'll see myself out." With that Annie handed Gwen the ring, stood up and walked out the front door, and back down the street to Grey Gables.

— 16 —

nnie was glad that she had the walk back to Grey Gables to cool down after what Gwen had told her. She decided not to tell Dervla anything about the conversation. It would only hurt her more than she had already been. Annie tried to think what she could do to set the record straight with Tony; even if she could contact him, how could she tell him that his mother had lied to him? She wondered if her friendship with Gwen could ever be repaired.

While Annie was at Wedgwood, Dervla had made her airline reservation. The best price she could get was a week from Tuesday, so she asked Annie if she could stay another week, and offered to pay for her room and board.

"Nonsense," said Annie, "I'd just keep you here if I could. It's been so much fun having another person in the house. I'm going to miss you when you go. You're always welcome here, Dervla, and I hope that someday you'll come and visit me again."

"Thanks, Annie," said Dervla. "I don't know what I would have done without you. I know there's a reason for everything that happens. Maybe our friendship was the plan all along. God moves in mysterious ways."

*   *   *   *

Andrew called Annie the next morning while Dervla was in the shower. Annie asked how he was feeling.

"I look terrible," said Andrew, "but I feel much better today. I slept almost all day yesterday. I'm over at the studio now. How is Dervla? Have you heard anything more from Tony Palmer?"

Annie thought it was only right that Andrew should know the complete situation, since it had led directly to his injuries, so she told him everything. He listened, saying little.

When she had filled him in on all the details, he said, "I'm sorry for Dervla's sake that it didn't work out, but she may be better off in the long run. She'll find someone who's right for her—I've no doubt about that." He paused and said, "The real reason I'm calling is to invite you and Dervla over to the studio for lunch today. Even though I'm pretty scary looking, I'm really fine, and I know you have a lot of questions about the photographs and what I told you about my family. I'd like to fill you and Dervla in on some other details. I've tidied the place up and ordered some takeout from Maplehurst's restaurant, so I promise it will be edible."

Annie laughed and said, "I'll check with Dervla, but I think we're both free."

"Great!" said Andrew. "Unless I hear otherwise, I'll see you both around noon."

*   *   *   *

At five minutes to twelve, Annie and Dervla arrived downtown and found a parking space not far from Dress to Impress. Annie led the way to the side door that Andrew had unlocked on Saturday night. He had told her there was a doorbell, and she located it and pushed it. She was just about to push it a second time when Andrew opened the door.

She almost gasped, and Dervla actually did when they saw him. The bruising on the left side of his face had spread and was more colorful than before—purple, blue, pink, green, and even yellow. It looked painful, and Andrew did wince a bit when he smiled and said, "Don't be concerned, ladies—it only hurts when I laugh."

Annie pretended to groan and said, "You mustn't be too bad off if you can make that old joke."

They followed him up the stairs into the studio. The window blinds on the north side of the room had been pulled up to let in the sunlight without too much brightness. The studio still had the look of creative chaos, but Andrew had straightened up the tables. One was covered with a white cloth and set with table service from Maplehurst Inn. He'd done more than order "takeout"—it looked like he had the waitstaff come over and set up a real dining experience. There was a salad at each place setting, a crusty loaf of French bread with a crock of creamy butter, and in the middle of the table was a covered tureen—the aroma coming from it was making Annie's mouth water.

"This is super, Andrew," said Annie. "I wasn't expecting such royal treatment."

"It's the least I can do for your kindness and cooperation since I've been here. I have to admit it's been a bit more ... uh ... adventurous? ... than I'm used to, but I can't say it hasn't been interesting."

Andrew looked pointedly at Dervla. "I wanted to thank you for being my model, Dervla. You were tremendously inspiring. The first time I saw you, I was a little … shocked, actually. I think you both noticed I wasn't quite myself. By way of explanation, there's something I'd like to show you."

Andrew walked over to the shelves that held his books and picked up five small volumes. All appeared to be the same size with green-leather covers and gold lettering on the spines. A couple of the books looked older, as if they had been looked at more, and the green leather was somewhat faded. Annie could see the front cover on the top book; it was embossed with a Celtic interlace pattern in the center. At the top there was the title in gold—*Mystic Verse,* and she could read the author's name below: Cara O'Connell. Andrew handed the books to Dervla.

She looked puzzled. "Why do you have copies of all my mother's poetry books?" she asked.

It was Annie's turn to be shocked.

"Open the top one," said Andrew.

Dervla opened the book and read aloud the inscription that was written on the title page. "To Andrew: Dear one, you've touched my life, and without your encouragement to follow my dreams, the book you hold in your hands would not have existed. Thank you. I wish you the best as you follow your dreams. I wish we could have followed that path together, but you are right—that life is not for me. I will love you always, Cara."

Dervla's eyes teared up as she read the words her mother had written.

Andrew said, "She sent it to me about a year after I had returned to the United States. I loved your mother, Dervla, but your father was the better man for her. I never met him, but I know she was happy. She sent me a note shortly after she married him. That was the last time I heard from her. I bought her other books myself, as my way to keep up with her from afar."

Annie asked if she could see the books. Only the top one said "Cara O'Connell"; the remaining four volumes showed the author's name as "Cara O'Keefe."

Andrew continued, "When I saw you at the top of the stairs, I only saw your mother's face, wearing a dress that looked so much like the one from my great-grandmother's photograph. I was so stunned—I thought you were a ghost! I know that sounds foolish, but in the moment it was all I could think."

"Why didn't you say something before?" asked Dervla.

"I wasn't sure how to tell you, and you seemed to have so much going on otherwise. But after all that's happened, and now—Annie says you're heading home next week—I couldn't let you go and not tell you. I hope we can spend some time together this week before you go. We can swap stories about your mother."

Dervla smiled. "I'd like that. Since my grandmother died, there's really been no one that I could talk with about her."

"That's settled then," said Andrew. "Now, I think we'd better have lunch before it gets cold."

The tureen held a flavorful bouillabaisse that all three enjoyed. Dervla seemed relaxed and talked at length about her mother, and her father too. Hearing about them helped

Annie see how much they had shaped her into the person she was. It made her wish that she had been able to know them. Andrew listened attentively, and his eyes seemed to mist a bit. Annie wasn't sure if it was because he was thinking about the past as it was, or because he was thinking about the road he hadn't chosen.

After lunch, Andrew showed Dervla the canvases he'd painted on Saturday since she hadn't had the opportunity to see them. Her reaction was almost identical to Annie's. Then he showed her Lydia Grey's baby picture and the wedding photograph that showed Amanda in the wedding dress.

"So, where did the crocheted trim, and the veil and the gloves come from?" Dervla asked.

"I wasn't sure until Annie told me about the label she found inside the dress with Amanda Grey's name and the year 1918 embroidered inside," said Andrew. "I think that she must have added the crocheted trim to the dress, and made the other items, with the intention that Lydia would wear them when she got married."

Annie started to say something, but Andrew began to fill in more details. "But Lydia didn't wear it. You see, she married Philip Randolph Gareth in 1918, shortly after he returned home from serving overseas during World War I …"

P.R.G.! The image of the hatbox flashed in Annie's mind. "And did Lydia Grey and Philip Gareth elope, by any chance?" asked Annie.

Andrew looked puzzled and started to say, "How did …" but broke off as if he realized what had happened. "You figured out the painting on the hatbox, too, didn't you?"

At this point, Dervla spoke up. "What do you mean 'figured it out'?" she asked.

Annie told them how she and Alice had used Betsy's flower books to decode the message of the bouquet on the hatbox, which had been painted, she now realized, by Andrew's grandfather, Philip Gareth.

"Did you know that your grandparents had eloped?" asked Annie.

"I did know. But I didn't know about the secret message that Philip had sent to Lydia, that is, until you pointed out my grandfather's initials on the lid of the hatbox. I know a good deal about the symbology of flowers—it's one of those things that, as an artist, I've studied. Once I knew the initials were there, it just sort of hit me all at once. It really caught me off guard. I don't think anyone else in the family knows about the hatbox."

"Do you have any idea why they eloped?" asked Annie.

"According to family lore, Lydia was the only child that Amanda and Zacharias were able to have, and they provided her with all the best that they had to offer. She was well-educated, and her parents' plan was that she would marry someone of the upper classes—wealthy, in other words. She was twenty years old when she met Philip Gareth. They fell in love, but he wasn't considered a good match. He was one of the Army Corp of Engineers artists who was sent to Europe to record the events of World War I in paintings. He was wounded and sent home a few months before the war ended. An injured Army veteran, whose main skill was artistry, didn't inspire a lot of confidence in his ability to support a wife in the manner to which she was accustomed in her parents' minds. But Lydia loved him, and he was hard-working and keen to make his mark in the world. Captain Grey told Lydia there would be long years of struggle ahead for Philip, and he didn't want that kind of life for his daughter. He forbade the marriage. But Lydia knew her heart and couldn't be deterred from following it. So, they eloped. The Captain refused to see them, and Lydia's mother, Amanda, conformed to the wishes of her husband."

"Why didn't she stand up to him?" asked Dervla. "I can't imagine refusing to see your own daughter. Did they never see her again?"

Andrew answered, "It was a different time, Dervla. Wives were expected to comply with the wishes of their husbands. Women didn't even have the right to vote yet, at least in this country. Amanda died the same year Philip and Lydia were married, and they moved to the other side of the country—out to Washington—not very long after that. I don't think they ever came back to Maine. It saddens me to think that Zacharias lived and died so alone when he could have been surrounded by his family—grandchildren and even a few great-grandchildren by that time.

Andrew looked at the photograph of his great-grandfather. "I haven't been able to find anyone still alive that knew my great-grandfather very well. There are people in Stony Point who knew of him, but it seems that not that long after Amanda died, he gave up seafaring altogether and closed himself off from other people."

"It's difficult when you see people just give up; makes you wonder what was going on inside his mind," said Annie.

"I guess we'll never know why he made the choices he

did," said Andrew. He paused for a moment and then asked, "Would you care to see photographs of Lydia and Philip?"

"Yes!" said Annie.

Reaching again into his bag, Andrew pulled out a small folded frame. Once opened, Annie could see in the left-side frame Philip Gareth, a solemn young man in a soldier's uniform, his jacket neatly buttoned up under his neck, and his sandy-color hair carefully parted on one side and combed down. In the right-side frame was a young woman with dark, upswept hair. Annie smiled when she saw the familiar dark eyes. She now saw clearly how much Andrew resembled his grandmother and his great-grandmother. That was the resemblance she had noticed when she looked at the second painting Andrew had made.

"Because they eloped, they didn't have a wedding picture made," said Andrew, "but these were taken near the time they were married."

Annie decided to share more of what she knew about Amanda Grey and her concern for her daughter. "There is something else that might help you to understand your great-grandmother better, Andrew," said Annie. Then she told Andrew and Dervla about the prayer that had been discovered when the veil was taken apart for cleaning, and that she had photographs of it.

"I don't think Amanda gave up on Lydia," Annie said, "but just put it in God's hands. She must have put the dress away after Lydia eloped, and it was left untouched at Grey Gables until Gram came across it and moved it to the mannequin where I found it. It belongs to you, Andrew—and your family. Just let me know when you want to take it, and the hatbox."

"Thanks, Annie. I'm sure that my family will want to see the dress and the painting on the hatbox." To Dervla he said, "I don't know what the future holds for you, but when you do get married someday, I hope you will still want to wear the wedding dress—it's perfect for you. ... And if you need someone to 'give you away,' I hope you'll think of me."

With that, Dervla gave him a big hug and said, "Thank you, Andrew. That means the world to me."

*   *   *   *

The next day, Annie entered A Stitch in Time just a few minutes before the Hook and Needle Club meeting was to begin. Gwen hadn't come, but the others were seated and working on their projects for the shower. Word had gotten around about the fight in Annie's front yard, and there were a lot of questions that she answered if she could and fended off if she felt it would only lead to more hard feelings or just be fodder for gossip. She didn't want to reveal what Gwen had told her; she hoped that somehow that rift could be mended, though she didn't see how. There was still no word from Tony Palmer.

Annie told the others that it appeared that the engagement was off and that Dervla was leaving in a week, but was still going to be in town on Saturday, the day they'd planned the hope-chest shower. Even though there might not be a wedding with Tony Palmer, she thought they might go ahead with the shower. The concept of a hope chest was still a good idea, even if a wedding was not in the immediate future. It would also be a nice way to say goodbye to Dervla.

The vote to go ahead with the shower was unanimous, and each member showed the work she had done on her gift.

Alice was making good progress on the ivory-color linen table topper she had planned out in the library at Grey Gables. She was embroidering the claddagh symbol using several shades of gold floss and the embellishments in the corners with various shades of green floss.

Stella was knitting a bed scarf—a smaller version of an afghan, made wide enough to cover the width of a bed but just tall enough to cover the area over the feet. The yarn was variegated in jewel-tone colors of blue, green, and violet. It was a bulky-weight yarn, and she was using large needles, so the project was progressing rapidly.

Kate was crocheting a lacy half-length vest from ivory-color fingering-weight yarn. The front and bottom edges had a woven pattern, like Celtic knot-work. She was nearly finished and explained to the group that she only had to add the collar. It was her own design, and to Annie it looked complicated, but Kate was an expert and it was amazing how quickly she could work. Kate told them that Mackenzie had stayed overnight with Vanessa over the weekend; they'd stayed up late watching movies and were able to each finish a pot holder and a dishcloth.

Mary Beth was working on a doily made of green variegated thread that featured shamrocks in repeating rounds. She told the group that if she finished this large one in time, she was going to use any remaining thread to make coasters to match.

Peggy had found a fabric panel for a wall quilt that was printed with the image of a Celtic cross. She had machine-sewn on borders, and was hand-quilting around the intricate details of the panel. She was glad that Emily was working on her woven pot holders in the evening, since it gave Peggy a chance to sit and get some quilting done.

Annie showed them the collar she was making, now half-finished. It had taken her a while to get used to the pattern stitch, and she'd had to pull it out a few times, but now she had gotten the hang of it and knew that she'd be able to get it finished in time.

Mary Beth reported that there had been no contact about the shower from Gwen, her daughter-in-law Sandra, or from Meredith. It was unlikely that any of them would attend, especially now that it appeared that the engagement was at an end.

Annie sighed. "I wish this could have all turned out differently."

"You haven't given up hope, have you Annie?" asked Mary Beth. "That doesn't sound like you."

Annie smiled. "No—I haven't given up hope. It's just that sometimes it's hard to see what good can come of things that have gone so wrong—at least in our eyes." Annie thought of the faith that Amanda had demonstrated when she crocheted her prayer into the veil, at a time when she must have felt that everything had gone wrong. "I guess it's natural to always want a happy ending to every story, but if life always turned out the way we wanted it to—or expected it to—we'd forget to practice faith in God and to turn to Him for all our cares. I need to remember that."

— 17 —

The day of the hope-chest shower, Annie enlisted Andrew's help to get Dervla out of Grey Gables so Annie could help Alice get things ready at the carriage house. He told Dervla he needed some research done and asked her to go to the library with him. He picked her up in the morning to take her to the library when it first opened. Andrew planned to take her out to lunch at Maplehurst Inn and asked Ian to join them for a leisurely meal. The shower was planned for two in the afternoon, and Annie had instructed him to bring Dervla back to Grey Gables about one thirty.

Annie and Alice spent the morning making sure the carriage house was extra spiffy. Annie always marveled at what a knack Alice had for decorating. The outside of the house had charming architectural details that were original to the building, but the interior would have been rather nondescript, except for the flair with which Alice had made it her own. Annie thought Alice would make a great interior designer, and sometimes told her she ought to open her own business.

Annie set up her laptop in Alice's living room so that she could display the photographs that Molly had taken of the wedding ensemble as a circulating slideshow. She especially wanted everyone to see the prayer that had been crocheted into the veil.

Alice had arranged to borrow a long folding table from the church hall so Annie helped her set it up at the end of the living room closest to the kitchen. While Alice made punch with raspberry sorbet and ginger ale, Annie covered the table with a pretty tablecloth and set out dessert plates, napkins, and flatware at one end, leaving space in the center for whatever dishes the other ladies were bringing. Alice would place the punch and cups at the opposite end of the table.

When that was finished, Annie went back to Grey Gables. She arranged a crudités plate with a bowl of dip in the center, and covered it all with plastic wrap. She had finished the collar the previous day and had wrapped it upstairs in her bedroom. She went to retrieve it, and then she carried her gift and the plate of crudités to the carriage house. Then she went home to shower and change. She didn't want to dress up too much—she wanted Dervla to be completely surprised. As promised, Andrew dropped Dervla back at Grey Gables half an hour before the other guests were scheduled to arrive.

Annie was supposed to keep Dervla occupied so that she wouldn't be looking out the window when the others came. They'd agreed that they would carpool as much as possible, stop at the carriage house to drop off their presents and finger foods, and then park their cars down the street and walk back to Alice's house. Annie asked Dervla to come into the library to show her Gram's scrapbook of all the cross-stitch patterns she'd designed. It was all Annie could think of to keep her busy. It worked fine since the samples were beautiful, and Dervla really was interested in seeing them.

At two o'clock, as arranged, Alice called Annie on the phone to let her know that all was ready. Annie walked back into the library where Dervla was still looking at the scrap-book and asked innocently, "Alice asked us down to the carriage house for a cup of tea—shall we go?"

"Sure," said Dervla, "that would be nice. I haven't been over to Alice's place yet."

Annie rang the doorbell when they arrived and stood to the side so that Dervla could go first. Alice opened the door, and Dervla stepped inside to the sound of "Surprise!"

"What's all this for?" she asked, laughing. "It's not my birthday, you know."

"We planned this for you," said Mary Beth. "We're call-ing it our 'hope-chest shower.' Do you know what a hope chest is?"

Dervla smiled, "Yes, we have that custom in my country too. I have my grandmother's old hope chest."

"Well, you'll have some new things to add to it when you get home," said Mary Beth.

"This is very kind of you," said Dervla. "You didn't have to do this, but thank you so much."

The noise level rose as everyone began talking. Vanessa introduced her friend Mackenzie to Dervla, and they both proceeded to inundate her with questions about Ireland.

Soon, the doorbell rang. Annie and Alice exchanged puz-zled looks. Everyone who was expected was already there. Alice opened the door. It was Gwen and her daughter-in-law Sandra. Sandra carried three prettily wrapped gifts, and Gwen balanced a large tray with different kinds of cookies.

Gwen seemed reticent, as if she wasn't sure how she

would be received. She may have thought that Annie had told everyone about their conversation on Sunday, but the only person she had told was Andrew. Not even Alice knew about the mistruths that Gwen had told Tony about Dervla and Andrew.

Alice asked the two ladies to come in and took the cookie tray to place on the food table. Peggy and Emily offered to take the gifts and place them with the others. Both Gwen and Sandra greeted Dervla; though the exchange seemed very awkward to everyone present, at least it was friendly. Alice carried in a couple more chairs from the back, and everyone was seated.

Alice handed out pencils and copies of the list of questions for the game she had described to the others when they were planning the shower. The room was mostly quiet while they filled out the questionnaires, except for the sound of Peggy's voice as she read each question to Emily so she could play too, or when Emily occasionally asked, "Mommy, how do you spell …?" When everyone was finished, Dervla read off her answers so each one could "grade" her answers. No one was surprised when the winner was Annie; after all, she had spent the most time with Dervla. Alice gave Annie her prize—a scented votive in a frosted-glass candleholder.

Next, Dervla began opening her presents. Mary Beth explained that all the gifts were homemade. Each one was appreciated and passed around the room so that everyone could look closer. One of the packages that Sandra had carried in was from Meredith. It contained a lovely crocheted ecru drawstring purse. Sandra had knitted a beautiful neck scarf in mint green with a repeating leaf pattern and long fringe on the ends. Gwen gave Dervla the Fair Isle pillow cover Annie had seen her working on at the Hook and Needle Club meeting before Tony and Dervla arrived from Ireland.

When she had finished opening all the presents, Dervla thanked everyone and said she would treasure each gift always. As the guest of honor, Alice asked Dervla to head the line at the food table. With snacks and punch to drink, everyone settled in to visit in the living room, except Vanessa and Mackenzie, who went with Emily into the kitchen so that she could have her snack at the kitchen table.

Annie took the opportunity to turn on her laptop to begin the slideshow of the wedding-dress photographs. Annie said, "I've uploaded the photographs that Molly Williams took of the wedding dress and the veil and gloves that I found in the attic, so that you all can see the details, including the labels and one other 'new' aspect that I was saving as a surprise." Then she explained how Molly had discovered Amanda's stitched prayer. As the pictures slowly changed on the screen, Annie told what she had learned from Andrew about the story of Zacharias and Amanda Grey, their daughter, Lydia, and of her elopement with Philip Gareth. Annie didn't think that Andrew would mind if she told them the other details he had shared about his family—that Lydia and Philip had moved to Washington and had had seven children, the youngest of which was Andrew's father. Lydia and Philip had lived happily together for over 50 years until Philip's death in the early 1970s.

"Just think," said Peggy, "her prayer has been there all this time, with no guarantee that anyone would ever find it."

"I think you're missing the point, Peggy," said Stella. "It's a prayer from Amanda to God, and He has always known that it is there. It's instructive to us now, as an example of faith—perhaps that's why Annie found it in the first place."

Annie smiled at Stella's wise observation.

Later on, the party began to break up. Mary Beth, Kate, and the teens came together in the same car and left first. Stella had told Jason to pick her up by four, and Peggy and Emily had gotten a ride with her, so they headed out as well.

Sandra had to drive back up to Portland and made a special effort to speak to Dervla before she left. "I hope I see you again, Dervla. I know that Gwen wants to talk to you. I hope everything will be straightened out."

Annie, Gwen, and Dervla were the only ones remaining and they set about helping Alice clean up everything and wash the dishes. When things were tidy again, Gwen asked Dervla if she could have a word with her in private.

Dervla looked at her friends and said, "If you don't mind, I don't have any secrets to keep from Annie and Alice. If you have something to say, I'd like them to hear it as well."

"Yes," said Gwen, "that's fine. I just wanted to apologize to you, Dervla. Please forgive me for not welcoming you as I should have and for refusing to get to know you. I was taken aback when you came home with Tony and he announced that you were engaged, but that is no excuse for treating you as I have."

Dervla said nothing. Gwen sighed deeply and looked down at the floor. "I've wronged you terribly, and I'm ashamed. I have to tell you that Tony did what he did—attacking that man—because of what I told him about you.

I told him you'd been seeing that artist, intimating that it was more than just friendship."

Dervla's shock clearly registered on her face. "Why would you do that? What have I done besides love your son?"

"I'm so sorry, Dervla!" said Gwen, with true remorse. "I know there's no excuse. My only thought was to stop him from getting married. I knew it was wrong. But I didn't imagine he would get so angry and actually become violent. He's never behaved that way before. Please believe me."

"I do believe you, Mrs. Palmer. I know that Tony is good. But you may have been right. I might not be good for him. I don't understand why he hasn't tried to speak to me or to contact me. If he asks, you may tell him that I'm flying back to Ireland on Tuesday."

"That's one of the reasons I'm here. I've been trying to call him all week, but he hasn't picked up his phone. Finally, he called me this morning. He is in Boston. That's where he went when he left Wedgwood. His new job started last Monday."

"He accepted a job in Boston?" asked Dervla.

"Yes, he was on his way to tell you on Saturday, but when I told him my stories, he became angry and stormed out of the house. I didn't know what had happened at Grey Gables until Annie told me on Sunday when she came to Wedgwood."

Dervla looked at Annie. "Why didn't you tell me you went to Wedgwood?"

"I didn't want to add any more stress to what you were already burdened with, Dervla," said Annie.

"It was good that you came over, Annie," said Gwen.

"I'm glad that you spoke to me the way that you did. I needed to hear it. I knew I had to tell Tony what I had done. When he called, I told him." Gwen was almost crying now. "He was so hurt that I had lied to him. I don't know if he will ever trust me again."

Dervla looked away. It seemed to Annie that she was torn between her anger at what Gwen had done and compassion for her.

Gwen composed herself somewhat and continued, "Tony is driving up to Stony Point tonight. He'd like to see you if you are willing, Dervla. What shall I tell him?"

"Tell him to call me on the phone at Grey Gables, and we'll talk," said Dervla.

Gwen left the carriage house to walk home to Wedgwood, and Annie and Dervla walked back to Grey Gables. Tony called later in the evening, and he and Dervla talked for over an hour. Afterward, Dervla told Annie that she had agreed to meet him on Sunday to see if they had any future together.

"I just don't know Annie. I want to be with him, but I don't know if it's the right thing to do," said Dervla. "Tony said he called Ian to ask him to set up a meeting with Andrew so that he could apologize and offer to pay Andrew's medical expenses. I'm glad to see him take responsibility for what he did. Even so, I don't know if I can ever forget how he attacked Andrew that day; even though I know the reason for it now, it doesn't change what he did."

"I wish I could tell you that everything will be perfect, but in truth, none of us knows what the future will bring," said Annie. "My only advice is to take your time. My tendency is to err on the side of love. If you love him—and I think you do—you can overcome a lot. Gwen has been a hurdle, but I think she learned something about herself, and you'll find she's very different than the person you've seen before today."

* * * *

Annie saw very little of Dervla on Sunday. Tony was at Grey Gables early in the morning to pick her up. Tony's face was slightly bruised too; there was a lingering mark along his jaw line. He was rather sheepish and apologized to Annie for his behavior. The confidence that he had exuded in her past contacts with him seemed to have been diminished. Annie wondered how long it would take for all the effects of Gwen's deception to wear off, or if, like a deep wound, there would always be scars.

That evening, Annie and Boots relaxed on the sofa, watching a movie on television—at least Annie was watching; Boots was more interested in relaxing. Annie had gotten out the baby afghan she had put aside when she was working on Dervla's present and proceeded to add more rows. During a break in the movie, she wandered into the kitchen to get some ice cream with Boots at her heels. Though the kitchen light was off, the room was quite bright. Annie walked to the window to see the full moon rising over the ocean. There was movement below on the beach that caught her eye, and she could make out the dark forms of two people standing close together, holding hands and looking at the moon. It was Tony and Dervla. Annie watched for a moment as they leaned together in a lingering kiss. Turning away from the window, Annie smiled and said to Boots, "It looks like there might be a wedding after all."

— Epilogue —

The October evening was clear and brisk, a gentle breeze rustling the multicolored leaves in the trees. Annie and Alice sat on the front porch of Grey Gables, each bundled up in a warm afghan. Mugs of hot tea helped make the cool night tolerable.

"Wasn't Dervla stunning today?" Annie asked Alice as they relaxed. Tony and Dervla's wedding had been held that Saturday morning in the chapel at Boothbay Harbor. It was followed by a huge reception at Maplehurst Inn, which had been arranged by Gwen and John Palmer. After the couple had departed for a brief honeymoon in New York City, and the crowd of well-wishers had begun to disperse, Annie and Alice decided to unwind back at Grey Gables.

"Yes," Alice agreed, "she was truly beautiful. Amanda Grey's wedding dress seemed destined to be worn by her."

"That was the feeling I had the first time I saw it on her," Annie said. "And I thought that Andrew 'giving away' Dervla completed the circle."

"It was a very touching service all-around," said Alice. "I did think that the matron of honor was also quite stunning," she teased. "You turned a few heads—especially one in particular—a well-known city official, I think."

"I don't know about that," Annie said with a hint of a smile. She had been pleased to have been asked to stand up with Dervla. She had to admit that Ian did seem to stick close to her side during the reception.

Annie's gaze turned out to sea, and her thoughts turned to the wedding dress, and Zacharias and Amanda Grey. "It's sad that Amanda never got to see her handiwork worn by her daughter, and that Zacharias, the man who built this lovely old home, never got to know his grandchildren because of the same stubbornness that Gwen displayed. I can't imagine never knowing John and Joanna."

"It is a tragedy in many ways," Alice said, "but fortunately, Gwen got it right in the end. I thought it might have ended when Dervla returned to Ireland, but it was a good idea for Gwen and John to go with Tony to Killarney when he asked Dervla to marry him the second time. And it was good to see Gwen being her old self at Hook and Needle Club meetings after she came back from their trip."

"And she loved Ireland so much!" Annie laughed. "I thought John was going to have to chain her to something in Wedgwood to keep her from going back."

She sipped her tea and thought again of the bitterness that had kept families separated. Stella had been right. The embroidered prayer from Amanda Grey to God had been answered in unexpected ways, but answered nevertheless. The wedding dress, the veil, and the gloves had, in their own way, brought reconciliation to a whole new generation.

Earlier that day, Annie had watched the wedding photographer record the wedding and the reception, capturing the bride and groom, and their guests, in all their finery. All around there had been smiles and laughter—a most joyous occasion. Thinking of that now, she remembered the photograph that Andrew had shown her of the Greys on their wedding day, and the pictures of his grandparents near the time they were married. She thought, too, of the photograph of her young and newly married parents that Dervla kept next to her bedside.

Now, in the chill of the autumn evening, Annie suddenly felt remarkably warm—and she smiled. In her heart of hearts she knew that somewhere Brian and Cara O'Keefe, Philip and Lydia Gareth, and Zacharias and Amanda Grey were united—basking in the love of Tony and Dervla.